THE JEWEL KINGDOM

Written by Jahnna N. Malcolm
Illustrated by Neal McPheeters

BACK**PACK**BOOKS
NEW YORK

2006 Backpack Books

ISBN-13: 978-0-7607-8145-6
ISBN-10: 0-7607-8145-1

Printed and bound in China

1 3 5 7 9 10 8 6 4 2

Table of Contents

❧

The Ruby Princess Runs Away

Table of Contents

Roxanne Runs Away

"I can't do it," Roxanne whispered from her hiding place in the royalberry tree. "I can't be a Jewel Princess. I'm not ready."

Today was the day she and her sisters would be crowned.

It was also the day they would leave the Jewel Palace where they had grown up.

As the Ruby Princess, Roxanne would have to move to her new castle in the Red Mountains. The mountains lay in the farthest corner of the Jewel Kingdom.

"I always knew this day would come," she murmured. "I just didn't think it would come so soon."

Roxanne stared glumly down at the palace courtyard. Creatures from every land were gathering there.

Sprites with blue skin and green hair chatted with goat-footed fauns. Richly dressed lords and ladies bowed to pointy-eared elves who rode on the shoulders of smiling giants.

"There you are!" A little red bird with a rainbow plume on its head fluttered onto the limb next to Roxanne. It was Twitter, the royal secretary.

"The king and queen have been looking for you!" Twitter squawked.

Queen Jemma and King Regal ruled the Jewel Kingdom. Today they were giving four of the Kingdom's lands to their daughters.

"Don't tell my parents where I am, Twitter," Roxanne pleaded. "I can't face them. Not yet."

"The ceremony is about to begin." Twitter tapped Roxanne's hand with his long yellow beak. "Everybody from the Jewel Kingdom is here."

Roxanne's big brown eyes widened. "Everybody?"

"Everybody who's anybody." Twitter ticked off the names of the guests on one wing. "There are the Gnomes, the Craghoppers, and the Pixies from the Red Mountains."

Roxanne gulped.

"Then there are all those creatures from the Greenwood, the Blue Lake, and the White Winterland."

Those were her sisters' lands.

"Then there are your cousins—"

"Stop!" Roxanne pinched Twitter's beak closed. "If you're trying to make me nervous," she whispered, "you are doing a very good job."

Twitter shook his beak free from her grasp. He hopped to the limb above Roxanne's head.

"You shouldn't be nervous," Twitter said. "You should be excited, like your sisters."

Roxanne's youngest sister Emily had been up since dawn, chattering about being crowned the Emerald Princess.

Demetra, the Diamond Princess, was the oldest of the four girls. She had spent the entire week in front of her mirror nervously weaving ribbons into her long brown hair.

Sabrina, the Sapphire Princess, was usually the quietest of the four. But even she had rattled on about Nymphs and Striders and all of the new friends she would make at the Blue Lake.

Every princess except Roxanne was happy.

"I just don't feel like a princess," she said with a huge sigh. "In fact, I feel very ordinary."

"Hush, my lady!" Twitter glanced nervously at the palace windows.

"Someone might hear you."

"But Twitter, look at me." Roxanne stood up in the crook of the tree. "I'm just a regular girl. I'm ten years old. I like to climb trees, ride horses, and go swimming."

"That will change," Twitter murmured.

"I don't like dresses." Roxanne gestured to her beautiful, red velvet gown. "I'd rather wear breeches."

Twitter winced. "Heaven forbid."

"And how can I rule and protect a whole kingdom of people, when I can't protect myself?"

Roxanne showed Twitter her leg. Her stockings were torn. And a very large lump had formed on her shin. "I banged my knee on the palace wall when I climbed up here."

Twitter fluttered in circles around the tree. "Oh, dear, oh, dear!"

Roxanne cocked her head. "How does a person rule, anyway?"

"How should I know?" Twitter ruffled his feathers. "You just order people around."

"Order people around." Roxanne wrinkled her nose. "That doesn't sound like fun."

"Who said being a princess was fun?" Twitter squawked.

Ta-ra ta-ra ta-ra!

The trumpets sounded at the front

gate. The palace herald announced, "Presenting the magnificent wizard Gallivant!"

"Gallivant!" Roxanne gasped, nearly falling out of the tree.

The wizard was very old and very powerful. Just hearing his name made Roxanne weak in the knees.

"There he is." Below her, Roxanne could see the big white plumes of the horses that pulled the wizard's gleaming glass coach.

Twitter flew to a ledge in the courtyard to get a closer look. He called to the princess, "Gallivant is carrying the Great Jewelled Crown!"

The crown held the jewels of the kingdom. It was written that whoever possessed these jewels would rule the land.

Roxanne watched everyone in the courtyard bow low as the wizard passed.

"Soon they'll be bowing to me," Roxanne murmured. "I'll be in a coach with the Ruby Crown on my head. The coach will take me far away from my parents and my sisters. And there I'll sit all by myself in some lonely old castle . . ."

Roxanne's voice trailed off. The palace gates were standing wide open.

Her eyes widened. *I don't have to be crowned today,* she thought. *I could just leap out of this tree and run away.*

Twitter flew back to her. "Hurry, my lady. You must join the king and queen and your sisters. They're about to greet the wizard."

Ta-ra ta-ra ta-ra!

The trumpets sounded again.

"It's now or never," Roxanne murmured, keeping her eyes fixed on the open gate.

Queen Jemma and King Regal stepped onto the marble steps of the palace. A cheer rang from every creature in the courtyard.

Roxanne gathered her skirts around her, took a deep breath, and leaped. "Now!"

2
Strangers on the Road

"Princess, stop!" Twitter cried. He flapped his wings, trying to keep up with Roxanne as she raced down the mountain. "Come back to the palace!"

Roxanne ignored Twitter. She was too busy trying to run and put on her cape. She had grabbed the cape from one of the ladies-in-waiting as she raced through the palace gates.

"If you won't come back, then I'm coming with you!" Twitter declared, flying in front of her.

"Suit yourself," Roxanne huffed. "But I want you to know I won't be going back. I'm through with being a princess."

"Do you know where you're going?" Twitter asked. "I mean, after all, you've never been far from the palace before."

Twitter was right. Roxanne had only left the grounds twice. Once, when she was a baby, traveling to Gallivant's Cave. And another time on a butterfly-watching trip with Queen Jemma.

"I've seen maps!" Roxanne declared. She pointed to a glistening ribbon of water that ran across the fields in front of them. "I know that's the Rushing River."

"It moves very fast and is often difficult to cross," Twitter pointed out.

Roxanne pointed to the gloomy stand of trees. It crept across the pastures like a big dark shadow. "That is the Mysterious Forest."

"Oooh," Twitter shuddered. "You want to stay away from there."

"Why?" Roxanne asked. "I've always been warned to keep away from the Mysterious Forest but no one has ever told me why."

"Because . . ." Twitter landed on her shoulder and whispered into her ear. "Because there is a secret passage in there. It leads straight to Castle Dread."

Roxanne's eyes widened. "Across the Black Sea? Where Lord Dread and the evil Darklings were sent?"

Twitter nodded.

Roxanne had often heard terrible stories of Lord Bleak. He had once ruled the Jewel Kingdom. But that was in the Dark Times, before Roxanne was born.

"Then I don't think we really need to go in the Mysterious Forest," she said in a shaky voice. "I say we head west."

"West is good," Twitter said, glancing nervously back toward the dark woods. "The Red Mountains lie to the west."

Roxanne walked toward the Rushing River. "There should be a stone bridge just over that rise. I remember it from the maps in Father's study. We can cross the river there."

But as they reached the bridge, two

figures in hooded black capes suddenly emerged from beneath it. They carried stout walking sticks and their hoods covered their faces.

"Where are you going, my pretty?" one of them asked in a crackly voice.

A chill ran down Roxanne's spine. She closed her cape to hide her red dress.

"That's really none of your business!" Twitter squawked from his perch on her shoulder.

"What an unusual creature," the other cloaked figure rasped. It stretched one bony finger toward Twitter. "The rainbow plume. Aren't those the palace colors?"

"Yes," Roxanne said quickly. "We're

on our way to the coronation."

"Oh, really?" The other stranger hobbled forward. "But the palace is behind you."

"My lady." Twitter pecked at Roxanne's shoulder. "My *lady*!"

She raised her hand to swat at the bird. "Twitter, please stop that!"

The hooded figures gasped. Roxanne realized they were staring at her gown.

One hissed to the other, "The Ruby Princess!"

Twitter tugged Roxanne away from them. "Th-th-these strangers," the bird stammered. "I think they may be D-d-dark—*awk*!"

His voice was cut off as a third

stranger appeared from the woods and grabbed him.

"Let go of him!" Roxanne ordered.

"Come and get him," the figure whispered.

"Run, my lady!" Twitter coughed.

Before Roxanne could make a move, a shadow darkened the sky above them.

Roxanne looked up.

A huge green creature with red scaly wings swooped toward her. It was breathing fire.

"By the Great Jewelled Crown," Roxanne cried as the creature plucked her off the ground with its claws. "A dragon!"

3

Hapgood the Dragon

"Permit me to introduce myself," the
dragon said when they were far away
from the hooded creatures. He gently
placed Roxanne on the ground. "My
name is Hapgood."

Roxanne was still a little rattled from
her quick flight through the air.
"Hapgood?"

The big green dragon nodded. He
tucked his wings into his body and
blinked his enormous blue eyes.

"But you may call me Happy," he said

in a very deep, very formal voice.

"My name is—" Roxanne's hand flew to her mouth. She couldn't tell this dragon who she really was. Roxanne the runaway princess.

But she didn't want to lie to him, either. After all, he'd just rescued her from the hooded strangers. So she said, "I am Roxanne. Of the Rushing River."

The dragon held out one claw. She shook it—carefully.

"Pleased to meet you, Roxanne," Hapgood said. Then he added, "Of the Rushing River."

Roxanne couldn't help staring at the marvelous creature.

"I've only met one dragon before," she

explained. "He was very fierce and spent a lot of time breathing fire. He burned up trees and chairs—anything made of wood. Are you fierce?"

The corners of Hapgood's mouth turned up in a smile. "I can be fierce when I want to be. But only when I meet creatures I don't like."

Roxanne looked back toward the bridge where the hooded strangers had tried to grab her. "I didn't like them one bit."

Hapgood's smile vanished and his eyes glowed red. "Those were Darklings. From Castle Dread. It's an ill sign when they appear in our kingdom."

"I wonder if Father—I mean, the

king—knows about them," Roxanne murmured.

"My lady!" Twitter squawked from above them.

The little red bird was out of breath. His feathers were ruffled. One of his rainbow plumes was bent.

He fluttered onto a limb beside Roxanne's head. "I thought you'd been kidnapped!"

"No, Twitter!" Roxanne laughed. "I'm quite safe. Meet Hapgood."

Twitter turned up his beak at the big green dragon. "We've met," he sniffed. "He nearly burned off half my feathers with that flame of his."

Hapgood bowed his head. "Please

accept my apologies. I was aiming for the Darklings."

Twitter's little black eyes widened. "I knew they were Darklings. Oh, this is not good. Not good at all."

Suddenly the ground began to tremble. The sound of hoofbeats filled the air. A man wearing the rainbow colors of the Jewel Palace galloped toward them.

"It's Armoral, captain of the palace guards!" Roxanne cried.

He'll recognize me for sure, she thought.

"Hide me!" she pleaded.

"Why? What have you done?" Hapgood asked.

Roxanne pursed her lips, trying to

think of something. "I, um . . . er, I . . ."

"She stole a banner from the palace courtyard," Twitter cut in. "She wanted a souvenir of the coronation."

Hapgood pulled a red and silver shield from under his wing. "Put this on your arm. It will make you and anyone you touch invisible."

Roxanne quickly strapped the shield to her arm. Then Twitter hopped onto her shoulder.

Hapgood whispered the magic words. "*Magic shield with power so bright, hide them from all others' sight.*"

Roxanne and Twitter disappeared.

"You there, dragon!" Armoral called, pulling his horse to a stop. "The Ruby

Princess has disappeared from the palace grounds. She was dressed all in red. Have you seen her pass this way?"

Roxanne squeezed her eyes shut tight. *Did Hapgood see my dress?* she wondered. *If he did, he'll know I'm the Ruby Princess.*

"No one has passed by me," Hapgood replied. "Do you think the princess was kidnapped?"

"The queen and king are certain of it," the captain said. "Queen Jemma is beside herself with worry."

Roxanne felt guilty. She hadn't meant to upset her parents.

"I think I saw a young girl in red clothes fishing by the stone bridge," Hapgood said.

"Thank you for that," Armoral barked. "I'll check the bridge."

Holding her breath, Roxanne listened to the fading sound of hoofbeats as the guard galloped away. Then she removed the shield and reappeared.

"It really works," she gasped to the dragon. "Armoral didn't see me or Twitter."

"No, he didn't," Hapgood replied. "But it wouldn't have mattered. He was looking for the Ruby Princess. And you aren't the Ruby Princess." He put his face right up to hers. "*Are* you?"

Roxanne swallowed hard. "No. I have not been crowned the Ruby Princess," she declared straight to Hapgood's face.

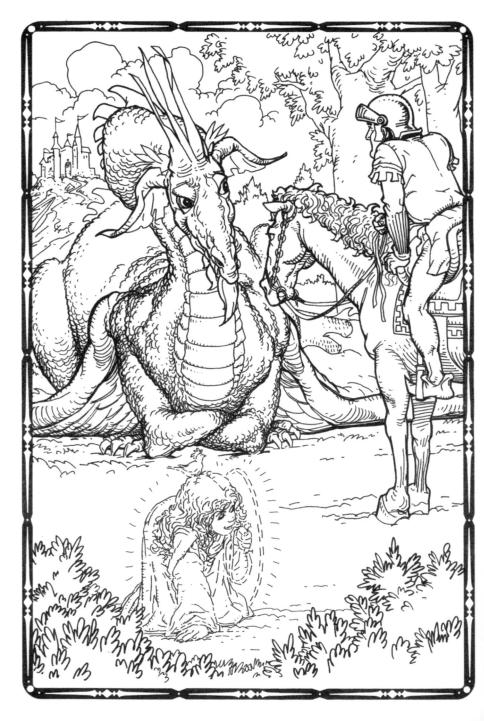

"I am Roxanne of the Running River."

"Didn't you say, *Rushing* River?" Hapgood asked, raising one eyebrow.

"I mean, the Rushing River," Roxanne said quickly. "I'm just a little nervous right now."

"Well, the captain has gone to look for the princess at the river's edge," Twitter pointed out. "You needn't worry about him."

"Hopefully he'll see the Darklings and tell the king about them," Roxanne murmured to Twitter.

She offered the magic shield to Hapgood. "Thank you for the use of this wonderful shield."

Hapgood held up one claw. "Keep it.

You may need it again. Remember, it has the power to make you invisible—but only for a short time."

"Someone's coming!" Twitter squawked. "Put on the shield."

Roxanne spun around as two squat figures hobbled toward them.

One was a little woman with fuzzy red hair and a round face. The other was a tiny man with a long gray beard. He was limping.

"Are they Darklings?" Roxanne asked Hapgood.

The dragon shook his head. "These are Gnomish folk from the Red Mountains."

Roxanne's eyes widened. That was to

be her new home. "The Red Mountains?"

"Yes." Hapgood frowned. "And they appear to be in trouble!"

4

Applesap and Marigold

"My name is Applesap," the little, bearded Gnome said. "And this is my wife, Marigold."

"We need help," Marigold cried. "We've been attacked."

"You're hurt!" Roxanne cried, kneeling beside the little man. "Your leg has a terrible gash on it."

Roxanne tore a strip of white cotton from her petticoat and handed it to Twitter. "Take this to the Rushing River. Dip it in the water and hurry back."

"Right away!" Twitter flapped off as fast as his wings would carry him.

Marigold had a scarf tied over her flaming-red hair. Her cheeks were dirty and streaked with tears.

"They came out of nowhere," she cried, burying her face in her hands. "And took everything we had."

"Who did this?" Hapgood boomed.

"Darklings," Applesap moaned.

"They're terrible creatures," Marigold said with a shiver. "Just terrible." She put her arm around her husband's shoulder and cried, "Poor Applesap."

Roxanne frowned. "Does your leg hurt much?"

"It's not my leg," Applesap said,

slumping down on a rock by the side of the road.

"It's his heart," Marigold murmured. "It's broken."

"You see, I'm a goldsmith," Applesap explained. "I was given the great honor of forging the crown for the Princess of the Red Mountains."

"The Ruby Princess?" Twitter asked, as he returned with the wet cloth.

Applesap nodded miserably. "I was bringing it to the great wizard Gallivant. He was to place the Ruby in it and crown our princess."

Roxanne's heart went out to the little Gnome. "Dear Mr. Applesap," she said, as she gently cleaned his wound with the wet cloth. "You can make another crown, just as fine as the first one."

"And I can fly you to the Jewel Palace," Hapgood offered.

"But I can't go to the palace empty-handed," Applesap said. "What would the princess think?"

"She would think you were a very sweet man who's had an awful experience," Roxanne replied. "And she would invite you to have a nice cup of wildroot tea with her."

Applesap laughed. "I wish."

"But you don't have to worry about that," Twitter cut in. "The princess has disappeared. Run away."

Marigold shook her head. "That's not

true. We saw the princess crossing Buttercup Meadow."

"What!" Roxanne and Twitter gasped.

"Marigold's right," Applesap said. "The princess was traveling in a beautiful glass coach. She was dressed all in red."

Marigold pointed to the hem of Roxanne's dress peeking out from under her cloak. "Like your dress there, Miss."

Roxanne leaped to her feet. "Are you sure about this?"

"Cross my heart," Marigold said.

"I even heard a knight in black armor cry, 'Make way for the Ruby Princess!'" Applesap said.

Roxanne turned to Hapgood. "We

have to go to the palace at once."

"But why?" Hapgood asked.

Roxanne tilted her chin high and declared, "Because that princess is an imposter!"

5

Imposter on the Throne!

Roxanne stared at the dragon and the
two little Gnomes. None of them had
moved a muscle.

"Didn't you hear what I said?" she
repeated. "That princess is not a real
princess."

"How—how do *you* know that?"
Marigold asked.

"Because . . . Because . . ." Roxanne
turned to Twitter for help.

"Because this lady is a friend of the
princess," Twitter explained quickly.

"That's right." Roxanne nodded. "We're the best of friends."

"And," Twitter continued, "she *knows* that the princess ran away."

Applesap squinted one eye shut. "But why would the princess want to run away?"

Roxanne took a deep breath. "You see . . . the princess told me she doesn't feel ready to rule the whole land. She doesn't know how."

Marigold and Applesap looked at each other and back at Roxanne.

"But I thought she was trained for that sort of thing," Applesap said.

"She was." Roxanne tore another strip of cloth from her petticoat as she explained, "The princess had her own tutor. They studied the Great Books telling of the Dark Times."

"Ah, yes." Hapgood nodded. "When Lord Bleak and the Darklings ruled our kingdom."

Roxanne tied the bandage around Applesap's leg. "The princess learned geography, too. She studied the kingdom's lands and the creatures that live in them."

"Did she learn to dance?" Marigold asked. "I love dancing."

"Oh, yes!" Roxanne giggled. "And how to sing, too."

"How nice," Marigold nodded pleasantly.

"She learned how to bow and look very regal," Roxanne finished. "But no one taught her how to rule."

Marigold shrugged. "If you ask me, ruling is very simple."

"All we ask is that our princess have a keen ear and a kind heart," Applesap said.

"So that she might hear our problems and help us solve them," Marigold added.

"That's all?" Roxanne asked. "That just sounds like a friend."

Marigold and Applesap smiled.

"That's right," Marigold said. "We would like the Ruby Princess to be our friend."

Roxanne looked confused. "But that's easy."

"For some," Hapgood observed. "But not for everyone."

Twitter fluttered anxiously overhead. "I hate to break up this tea party," he cut in. "But someone *really* must go to the palace. We have to stop them from crowning the wrong princess."

"I'll go!" Hapgood cried, raising up on his hind legs. "And I'll take all of you with me. Hop on my back."

Marigold helped Applesap to his feet. The two Gnomes climbed carefully onto the dragon's shoulders.

Roxanne frowned. "There really isn't room for all four of us."

"Then I'll stay," Applesap declared. "And you go. My leg feels much better, thanks to you."

Roxanne was torn. She knew she should go to the palace immediately. But Applesap was hurt. They couldn't leave him on the road. What if the Darklings came back?

"Applesap, you're hurt," Roxanne finally said. "You should ride. And Marigold, you should go with your husband. I can follow on foot."

"Then I'll travel with you," Twitter said, hopping off Hapgood's neck.

"I'll take Applesap and Marigold to the palace," the dragon said. "But how can we stop the coronation?"

"You don't need to stop it," Roxanne said. "Just delay it. I'll bring proof that she is a fake."

"We'll do our best." Hapgood unfurled his mighty red wings. "Be careful, Lady Roxanne of the Rushing River."

Roxanne placed one hand over her heart. "I'll be very careful."

With a swoosh, Hapgood rose into the air. "And if anything unpleasant happens, use the magic shield."

Roxanne waved at the two Gnomes clinging to the dragon's neck. "I'll see you all at the Jewel Palace."

Hapgood wheeled in a circle and ordered, "Take the short cut."

"Where is it?" Twitter called.

The dragon boomed a reply that Roxanne did not want to hear.

"Through the Mysterious Forest!"

6

The Mysterious Forest

Roxanne and Twitter followed a winding path deep into the Mysterious Forest. It was darker and colder than Roxanne had ever imagined.

"Twitter?" Roxanne whispered.

"Yes, my lady?" Twitter whispered back. He was riding on her shoulder.

"I'm scared."

"If it makes you feel any better," Twitter replied, "so am I." He held up a wing. "My feathers are shaking."

The trees in the forest were black and

twisted. The bushes were covered with long thorns. The smell of rotting leaves hung in the air.

A thorny branch reached out and tore Roxanne's skirt.

"Help!" Roxanne squeaked. "That bush tried to grab me."

"I wish we'd taken the long route," Twitter muttered. "I don't like this place one bit. It feels evil."

"It is," Roxanne said with a gulp. "Hapgood says there is a path here that leads directly to Castle Dread. Across the Black Sea."

"I don't doubt it." Twitter pecked Roxanne on the top of the head. "Walk faster, would you?"

Roxanne tried to go faster. But every step was hard. Thick roots tripped her feet. Black vines dropped from above and pulled at her hair.

Suddenly she stopped dead still.

"What is it?" Twitter asked. "Why are we stopping?"

"Voices," Roxanne whispered. "I hear voices. Just around that blackthorn bush."

"I'll go see." Twitter left Roxanne's shoulder. He flew to the bend in the path.

All of Twitter's feathers stood on end. He opened his beak but no sound came out.

"What is it, Twitter?" Roxanne

whispered, creeping up beside him.

"Those Darklings!" he croaked. "The three from the bridge. They're camped ahead. Turn back!"

"We can't, Twitter. We have to get to the palace."

"But the Darklings," Twitter peeped. "They'll stop us."

Roxanne remembered the shield Hapgood had given her. "Not if they can't see us."

"What do you mean?" Twitter asked.

Roxanne held up the shield and smiled. "We'll hide, Twitter. Hop on my shoulder. We'll be invisible."

Once Twitter was on her shoulder, Roxanne held the shield in front of her and murmured the words Hapgood had taught her:

Magic shield with power so bright,
Hide us from all others' sight.

"Now let's go," she whispered.

Twitter tapped her cheek. "Be careful, Princess."

Three Darklings in black capes were huddled around a map.

Roxanne started to tiptoe past, but something they said stopped her.

"Our plan is working perfectly," the leader said in a deep voice.

"Can you believe our good luck?" the shortest one snorted. "We were supposed to kidnap Princess Roxanne but she saved us the trouble by running away."

The third one laughed hoarsely. "With the real Roxanne out of the way, we can put our own princess on the throne."

"Our princess is already at the palace. I sent the carriage there myself," the shortest Darkling declared.

"Have you taken care of the shape-changing mask?" the leader asked.

"Yes. Princess Rudgrin is wearing it. She is Roxanne's mirror image."

"Rudgrin?" Roxanne whispered to Twitter. "Isn't she the daughter of Lord Bleak? I thought they were banished from our kingdom forever."

"They were," Twitter replied. "All the Darklings were. But it looks like they're back."

"With Rudgrin securely on the throne in the Red Mountains," the Darkling leader said, "we can then replace the other princesses, one by one."

Roxanne's eyes widened. "They plan to take over the Jewel Kingdom!"

"Oh, dear! Oh, dear! We have to keep them from leaving the forest," Twitter fretted. "But how?"

Roxanne looked around the Darklings' campsite.

Two giant roothogs and a gray-winged Gorax were tied at the edge of the clearing. The roothogs were pulling up the roots of some blackthorn bushes with their tusks.

"I've got an idea," Roxanne said.

"What is it?"

"Those two roothogs and that Gorax must be their rides," Roxanne whispered. "If we can tie the bird and the hogs to each other, then we can stall the Darklings."

"And that will give us enough time to run to the palace for help," Twitter whispered.

"Exactly," Roxanne replied. "But we better hurry. I don't know how long this shield will hide us."

Roxanne slipped as silently as she could through the thick brush, grabbing a rope from beside the Darklings.

She tied the first roothog's reins to the other roothog.

Then she made a large loop and swung that over the Gorax's head.

Grrawk! The bird shrieked as the rope tightened around its neck.

Roxanne froze.

"What was that?" The tallest Darkling spun to look at the bird.

For the first time, Roxanne got a glimpse of a Darkling's face.

It was hideous. His face was twisted in a permanent scowl. His eyes were two black holes. His teeth were short and pointed.

Roxanne shut her eyes, remembering

what her tutor had told her about the Darklings. *They were once a handsome people. But the evil inside them was so strong, it warped their features. Now they are as ugly outside as they are inside.*

Roxanne shivered. What if these terrible creatures really did take over the Jewel Kingdom? They would make it a horrible place to live. And it would be all her fault!

"I won't let that happen!" she declared to herself.

"What's that?" the leader asked the other Darklings. "Did one of you speak?"

"It must have been the Gorax," the short Darkling replied. "She hasn't been the same since we crossed the Black Sea."

"Back to our plan," the leader said, rolling up the map. "With Rudgrin safely on the throne, there is only one thing left to do. Find the real Ruby Princess and take her back to Castle Dread."

"Never!" Roxanne blurted out.

The Darklings turned just as the shield's magic wore off.

"Well, look who's here!" the leader hissed. "We're in luck!"

"Twitter," Roxanne cried. "We're no longer invisible."

"What do we do?" Twitter squawked.

"Run!"

7

Fly to the Palace!

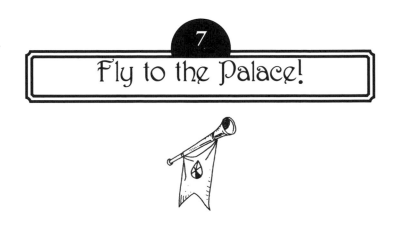

"Seize her!"

Two Darklings lunged for Roxanne. She fell backward into the Gorax.

"Twitter!" Roxanne cried. "I have an idea."

She leaped onto the Gorax and nudged its sides with her heels.

"Fly!" she ordered.

The Gorax croaked. With a heavy flapping of its gray wings, it lifted her off the ground.

"Stop!" the Darklings shrieked,

leaping onto the roothogs.

"The bird is tied to the roothogs," Twitter cried. "She's lifting them off the ground!"

"Higher!" Roxanne urged the Gorax. The great bird dragged the hogs and riders into the top branches of a tree.

"They're all tangled up!" Twitter reported with glee.

"Cut the rope!" Roxanne ordered. "Or we'll be pulled back down."

"Leave it to me!" With a sharp *rat-a-tat* of his beak, Twitter sliced the rope in two.

"Yes!" Roxanne cried, as the Gorax flew out of the trees. She prodded the Gorax with her heels and commanded, "To the palace!"

"Well done, my lady!" Twitter cheered, as they swooped out of the Mysterious Forest and flew toward the palace.

Roxanne wanted to smile. But she couldn't.

"We can't celebrate yet, Twitter. We still have to stop Rudgrin!"

When they reached the palace gates, Roxanne saw two tiny figures waving frantically.

"It's Applesap and Marigold!" she shouted. "Down, Gorax!"

The beast obediently glided to a halt near the waiting Gnomes.

"Thank heavens you're here," Applesap cried, as he limped forward. "Marigold and I tried to delay the crowning but they wouldn't listen to us."

"We told them about the Darklings stealing our crown," Marigold wailed. "But they insisted they already had the crown."

"And they do!" Applesap said. "The one the Darklings stole from me."

"Where's Hapgood?" Roxanne asked.

"He went back to look for you," Marigold said.

Ta-ra ta-ra ta-ra!

"Trumpets!" Twitter gasped. "They signal the coronation of the princesses. Oh, no! We're too late!"

"Not if I have anything to say about it!" Roxanne leaped off the Gorax and dashed up the palace steps.

When she reached the throne room, Roxanne clasped the jeweled door handles with both hands and took a deep breath. "Here goes!"

She threw open the doors. The great wizard Gallivant had already crowned Roxanne's three sisters. Now he was presenting the Ruby Crown to Princess Rudgrin.

Roxanne's velvet gown was torn. Her hair was tangled with blackthorns. But she knew who she was and announced it in a loud, clear voice.

"I am Princess Roxanne, the Ruby Princess of the Jewel Kingdom, ruler of the Red Mountains," she cried. "And I command you to *stop*!"

A Princess at Last

The Emerald Princess, the Sapphire
Princess, and the Diamond Princess
turned and stared.

The guests of the court stared.

Even King Regal and Queen Jemma
were staring.

First at Roxanne. Then at the girl who
sat on the throne.

"They're identical!" Queen Jemma
cried.

"That girl is an imposter!" Roxanne
declared. "She is Rudgrin, Lord Bleak's

daughter from Castle Dread."

Princess Sabrina and Princess Emily gasped at the mention of the Darkling lord. Princess Demetra nearly fainted.

"If this is true, why does she look like my daughter?" King Regal demanded.

"Because Rudgrin is wearing a mask," Roxanne replied.

"Guards!" Rudgrin shrieked. "Arrest her." She pointed at Roxanne. "*She's* the imposter."

Roxanne put both hands on her hips. "*You* are a *liar.*"

"Oh dear," Queen Jemma cried. "Whatever shall we do?" She turned to Rudgrin. "This Roxanne certainly looks like my daughter."

Then the queen faced Roxanne. "But this one, with the torn dress and messy hair, *acts* like my daughter."

Gallivant stepped forward. "There is only one way to find out who is the true Ruby Princess."

"How?" King Regal asked.

Gallivant fixed his stern gaze on Roxanne and Rudgrin. "Which of you bears the sign?"

"Sign?" Rudgrin repeated. "What sign?"

"The mark of the Jewel Princess," Gallivant boomed. "It is something every princess is born with."

Roxanne smiled first at her sisters and then at the wizard.

"I bear the mark," she said, stepping forward.

She raised her right arm and carefully turned back the cuff of her sleeve. There, for all the world to see, was a ruby teardrop on her wrist.

"The mark in the shape of her Ruby!" Gallivant declared. "She who bears the mark will wear the crown."

Then Emily, Demetra, and Sabrina raised their wrists. They, too, had a mark in the shape of their jewel.

Suddenly their crowns began to gleam.

"Look!" a lady-in-waiting gasped. "The jewels! They're glowing."

Twitter, who had been hiding behind

Roxanne, fluttered to Rudgrin. "You fake! Take off your mask."

"Noooo!" howled Rudgrin, as Twitter peeled off her mask with his beak.

The court gasped in horror when her twisted ugly face was revealed.

In the blink of an eye, Rudgrin was whisked out of the throne room by the palace guards. And Roxanne was ushered to the king and queen's side.

"I am so sorry," Roxanne said, hugging her mother and father tightly. "I nearly ruined everything."

Queen Jemma smoothed Roxanne's hair. "We're just glad to know you're safe."

Roxanne took her place beside her sisters. Sabrina blew her a kiss. Demetra squeezed her hand. "Welcome back," Emily whispered.

Now it was time for Roxanne to be crowned.

King Regal nodded to Gallivant, who signaled the court musicians.

Beautiful music filled the air.

Gallivant turned to the crowd. "The people of the Red Mountains have chosen one of their own to place the Ruby Crown on Princess Roxanne's head. Will he please come forward?"

There was a loud flapping and the room was filled with smoke.

Gallivant announced, "May I present—"

"Happy!" Roxanne cried with glee.

Ignoring all royal manners, she raced to greet her friend. "It's you!"

Hapgood folded his wings to his side and bowed low. "Greetings, Princess Roxanne of the Red Mountains." He winked and added, "And the Rushing River."

Roxanne wrapped her arms around his neck and whispered, "You must have known who I was all along."

"Yes, my lady," Hapgood confessed, sheepishly. "I did. When you ran away, Gallivant gave me the shield and sent me to find you."

Gallivant then presented the Ruby Crown to Hapgood. The dragon raised it above Roxanne's head.

"Wait!" Roxanne cried, stopping the ceremony. "I would like the man who forged this beautiful crown to be by my side." She searched the room for the bearded Gnome.

Applesap and Marigold stood at the back of the hall, looking very embarrassed.

"Come forward, friends," Roxanne cried. "And join the celebration."

Marigold, Applesap, and Twitter approached the throne.

Then Hapgood set the glittering Ruby Crown on Roxanne's head. "From this moment, I vow to be your friend and protector for all the days of my life."

Tears of joy shone in Roxanne's eyes.

She hugged and kissed each one of her sisters.

Then the new Ruby Princess turned to face the court. "As the ruler of the Red Mountains, I vow to have a keen ear and a kind heart, that I might always be a loving and giving . . . friend."

The Sapphire Princess
Meets a Monster

Table of Contents

1

The Golden Gift

"It's a perfect day for a picnic!" Princess Sabrina said, as she sailed across Blue Lake. She was riding in her laurel-leaf boat.

Gurt the Gilliwag sat behind her, paddling the boat. The green froglike creature was a close friend of the Sapphire Princess.

"My dear lady," Gurt said in his deep voice, "this very golden afternoon matches your golden gift."

That morning a golden basket had

mysteriously arrived at the gates of the Sapphire Palace. A card was pinned to the basket. It read, *To the Sapphire Princess. Signed, A Secret Admirer.*

The golden basket was filled with bread, cheese, and chocolate. Each piece was wrapped in gold cloth and tied with a sapphire-blue ribbon.

Princess Sabrina loved the basket. She invited her three sisters to join her for a picnic that afternoon.

Demetra, the Diamond Princess, and Emily, the Emerald Princess, had arrived. While they waited for the Ruby Princess, the three sisters sailed across the lake to Bluebonnet Falls.

"Let's have a race!" Sabrina called to

the Emerald Princess. Emily was on her knees, paddling a large green lily pad.

"I'm ready when you are," Princess Emily said, as she pulled up next to Sabrina. "Just say the word."

Of the four Jewel Princesses, Emily was the most athletic. She ruled the Greenwood and spent her days climbing trees and riding horses through her lush green forest.

The Diamond Princess steered her boat made of white gardenias between her two sisters. Demetra ruled the White Winterland and everything she wore was a glittering white.

"Let's wait for Roxanne," Demetra advised. "Wasn't she going to join us?"

"Roxanne is always late," Emily said with a frown. "If we wait for her, it will be sundown before we get to eat."

Sabrina focused her pale blue eyes on the shore. There was no sight of her sister Roxanne.

"I agree with Emily," Sabrina announced, tossing her long blond hair over her shoulders. "Let's have the race ourselves."

"No, no, no!" a yellow and pink butterfly squeaked as it landed on Sabrina's finger. It was Zazz, Princess Sabrina's palace advisor and best friend.

"Princess, if you race in this boat, you'll lose," Zazz sputtered. "Or sink. Just look at what we're carrying. Gurt.

That heavy gold basket. The napkins and tablecloths, and all of the royal china."

Sabrina put her face nose-to-nose with the tiny butterfly. "Then I'll just have to get another boat. Any idea where I might find one?"

Blue Lake was dotted with boats. "I'll call the Nymphs," Zazz said, as she fluttered off the princess's finger. "They'll bring a leaf boat right over."

"Don't do that," Emily called. "Sabrina, hop on my lily pad. We'll race Demetra together."

Sabrina stood up to leap onto Emily's boat, but something tugged at her arm.

Sabrina spun around. No one was

there. Just Gurt the Gilliwag calmly paddling away. She looked at the mysterious golden basket. It glittered in the afternoon sun.

"Come on, Sabrina!" Emily cried. "Jump!"

Before Sabrina could make a move, the basket danced across the bottom of the boat and leaped into her hands.

"Did you see that?" Emily gasped to Demetra.

"I don't like this one bit," Demetra said, shaking her thick brown braid. "Sabrina, you should leave that basket alone. You don't know where it came from."

"Don't be such a worrywart!" Sabrina stared at the golden basket. "This is a present. A very magical present from a secret admirer. Full of wonderful food."

"And I'm starving," Zazz called from her perch on the boat's bow.

"Me, too." Sabrina leaned forward and whispered to the butterfly, "Zazz, let's not wait until we get to Bluebonnet Falls. Why don't you and I take a piece of chocolate from the picnic basket right now?"

Zazz rubbed her little hands together. "I like chocolate. Yes, yes!"

Sabrina opened the basket. But just as her fingers touched the food, something jolted the boat.

"Whoa!" Zazz fell backwards onto the floor of the boat and bent one antenna. "What was that?"

"I'm not sure!" Sabrina replied.

Thunk!

Something hit the boat again.

"I'm afraid something is trying to sink us," Gurt declared, pulling his paddle into the boat.

"The Water Sprites must be playing a joke." Sabrina peered into the water. She was looking for the ghostly outline of the little sprites.

"If the Sprites don't want you to see them, Princess, you won't," Zazz said, as she tried to straighten her antenna.

"I'll try calling them." Sabrina cupped her hands around her mouth. "Hello? Anybody there?"

Nothing.

The Sapphire Princess leaned over the side of the boat. She was so close, her nose nearly touched the lake.

All at once two huge yellow eyes appeared just below the surface.

Sabrina screamed and fell backward in a faint.

2

The Blue Lake Monster

"Sabrina, wake up!" Demetra fanned Sabrina's face with a broad green leaf.

Zazz fluttered nervously over their heads.

"Is the Princess all right?" the butterfly asked.

Gurt pointed toward the palace. "Should I swim for help?"

"No, wait!" Princess Emily scooped a handful of ice-cold water from the lake. She tossed the water onto Sabrina's face. "Sabrina, open your eyes!"

Her eyelids fluttered open. "A face," Sabrina gasped. "I saw a face as big as this boat. It was under the water."

"I'll see what it was!" Gurt cried. The Gilliwag dove over the side and instantly disappeared from sight.

Demetra poured Sabrina a cup of honey nectar. "What did the face look like?"

Sabrina took the cup and slowly sat up. "Well, it was huge and gray. And very lumpy."

"Did it have a mouth?" Emily asked.

Sabrina nodded. "Yes. And its teeth looked razor sharp."

"What about the body?" Zazz asked. "Did you see it?"

Sabrina sipped the nectar. "I didn't see its body, but if its head was as big as this boat, then the body would have to be as big as ten boats."

Zazz frowned. "There's nothing that big that lives in the lake except . . ." Her eyes widened. "The Blue Lake Monster!"

They heard a splash behind them and everyone jumped. The Gilliwag draped his long green arms over the side.

"I saw a shadow," Gurt gasped. "I tried to follow, but it disappeared into the Deep Dark."

The Deep Dark was an inky stretch of water where none of the lake folk ever swam. It was very deep, black as night, and very, very cold.

Now Zazz's eyes were as huge as lily pads. "Then it *was* the Blue Lake Monster!"

Sabrina tapped Zazz on the top of the head with her fingertip. "What's all this talk about a Blue Lake Monster? I've never heard of it."

Zazz shivered. "It's terrible. Just terrible."

"The Monster has always been down there," Gurt explained. "Some say it is an evil demon left over from when Lord Bleak ruled the land."

"Lord Bleak!" Demetra gasped. "How awful!"

Lord Bleak and his Darklings had been banished from the Jewel Kingdom years before. That was when Queen Jemma and King Regal had come to the throne. They had divided up the Jewel Kingdom, giving each of their daughters her own jewel and her own land.

"If it has anything to do with Lord Bleak, it must be mean and horrible," Emily said, clutching her sisters' hands.

Gurt shrugged. "I don't know. I've never heard of the monster harming anyone."

"Then maybe it's a friendly monster," Sabrina said.

Zazz put her face close to Sabrina's. "But you said that it was gray and had fierce teech. Something that ugly has to be bad."

"I think you should warn your people," Demetra advised.

Sabrina didn't like to jump to conclusions. She preferred to think things over before taking any action. "I just saw a face," she said. "It could have been a Sprite playing a trick, trying to scare us."

Zazz reluctantly agreed. "They have been known to do that."

Sabrina smiled at her sisters and friends. "We're almost to Bluebonnet Falls. We were going on a picnic. So why don't we eat our lunch and talk about it?"

She picked up the picnic basket and set it in her lap.

Suddenly a huge gray head burst out of the water.

"The Blue Lake Monster!" Zazz squealed.

The monster opened its jaws and let loose a terrible roar.

Sabrina reached for her purse. Inside was magic dust that the great wizard Gallivant had given her. She tossed the dust over herself and her guests.

"*From Water to Air*," she chanted.

Sabrina, Emily, Demetra and Gurt instantly rose into the sky. Zazz fluttered beside them.

Sabrina extended one arm to the heavens. "*Higher and higher, let us go.*"

The group flew far above the monster's head. From her place in the

sky, Sabrina could see the dark shadow of the monster beneath the water. The creature was bigger than she ever imagined. Its body seemed to stretch halfway cross the lake.

"What shall we do, Princess Sabrina?" Zazz cried. "Where shall we go?"

Sabrina faced her palace, which sat like a bridge over Blue Lake. "Demetra and Emily, fly back to my palace with Gurt. Zazz, come with me."

"But where will you go?" Demetra asked.

Sabrina pointed to the far shore of Blue Lake. "To the Storkz. They'll know what to do!"

3

Call The Storkz!

The Storkz lived in Misty Marsh. It was always damp and always covered in a pale green cloud.

"Sage is the leader of the Storkz," Sabrina said, as they glided into the marsh. "We need to talk to him."

Zazz clung to the sleeve of Sabrina's gown. "I hope we find him soon," the butterfly mumbled. "It's cold and scary here. I can't see two feet in front of me."

"Don't worry, friend," Sabrina cooed. "There's nothing to fear."

Suddenly a creature with long yellow legs and a thin body covered in blue feathers magically appeared out of the mist. Its big round eyes peered at them from behind tiny gold-rimmed glasses.

"*Sage!*" Sabrina gasped.

"Have you been there all along?" Zazz squeaked, hopping to Sabrina's shoulder. "I didn't see you."

"We are all here." Sage gestured with one wing to the clumps of reeds around him.

Suddenly Sabrina could see dozens of Storkz. All standing tall and still.

"We hear through the waters that you are worried about our Lake Creature," Sage said, staring at her solemnly.

"That's no creature," Zazz cut in. "It's a terrible monster."

"Zazz!" Sabrina tapped the butterfly lightly on her head. "Careful what you say. We're not sure it's terrible."

"The Princess is right," Sage advised. "Let us not be too hasty. That creature has lived in Blue Lake a very long time."

"Is it older than the Storkz?" Zazz asked, wide-eyed.

Sage nodded. "Much older. It's been here since the beginning."

"That's why it's so big," Zazz whispered. "With all of that time, what else was there to do but grow!"

"This creature has never shown itself to humans before." Sage peered over the

top of his glasses. "There must be a reason for this."

"Of course there's a reason," Zazz sputtered. "That awful monster has been sent by Lord Bleak to hurt our princess."

Sabrina wanted to say that wasn't true. But she had to admit, the creature *did* frighten her.

"It attacked my boat," Sabrina told Sage. "And then it leaped out of the water and roared at me."

"Hmm . . . . This is not good," Sage murmured. "I must talk to the Storkz."

In an instant, all of the pale blue birds vanished from sight.

"Do you think the Storkz are still here?" Zazz whispered.

"Yes," Sabrina whispered back. "I can't see them, but I can feel them all around us."

"Go back to your palace, Princess," Sage said when he returned. "We will try to speak to the Lake Creature."

Sabrina bowed to the leader of the Storkz. "Thank you. I will do as you say."

"What do you mean, you'll do as he says?" Zazz demanded, as they flew back to the Blue Palace. "Sage just wants us to sit and wait!"

"We must be sure about this creature before we scare our people," Sabrina explained. "Promise me, Zazz, that you'll keep this secret."

"Too late," the butterfly said, as the palace came into view. "It looks like the secret is out."

Sabrina looked down. The shallow water around the palace was crowded with blue-skinned Nymphs and gawky Gilliwags. They waved huge willow wands in the air. Big-footed Striders skated under the drawbridge, clutching oars in their hands. Even the Water Sprites, pale and ghostlike, had joined the mob.

"We must all hunt for this monster!" Gurt shouted from the center of the crowd.

"Find the monster!" the crowd shouted back.

"And when we find this beast," Gurt added, "we must kill it!"

Fear gripped Sabrina as the mob howled, "Kill the beast!"

Princess Sabrina and her sisters huddled
together by her bedroom window. Below
they could see the crowd guarding the
palace.

"It's very sweet that my people want
to protect me," Sabrina remarked. "But
I'm worried."

"I'm worried, too," Princess Demetra
said. "That monster could destroy all of
those willow wands with one swift bite."

Sabrina leaned her head against the
frame of her open window. She thought

about what Sage had told her.

"Why would this monster, who has lived peacefully for so many years, suddenly appear?" she asked her sisters.

"Maybe it wants to tell you something," Emily suggested.

Sabrina nodded. "That's what I've been thinking. But what?"

"I think it wants you to go home. Back to the Jewel Palace," Demetra said. "And that's what I would do if I were you."

Sabrina squeezed her sister's hand. "I can't leave, Demetra. This is my land. When I was crowned Sapphire Princess, I promised to protect Blue Lake and all of the creatures who live here."

"Even *that* creature?" Emily pointed at the lake. Just below the surface, as big as a ship, was the Blue Lake Monster!

Demetra backed away from the window. "Sabrina, I'm scared! Why has it come to the palace?"

Sabrina watched the shadow glide swiftly toward the drawbridge. "It's after my people," she gasped. "I've got to stop it!"

"But how?" Emily cried. "You're just one little girl. And that thing is monstrous."

"I have to do something." Sabrina climbed onto the window ledge and peered out. "The Gilliwags and the Nymphs don't even see it!"

Emily caught hold of Sabrina's ankle. "Careful, sister, you might fall."

Sabrina's big blue eyes widened. "That's it," she said. "I'll leap out of my window and distract it."

"But it will gobble you whole," Demetra warned.

"I won't land in the water." Sabrina patted the purse at her waist. "I'll use my magic dust and fly across the lake."

"Then the monster will follow you," Emily said.

Sabrina smiled. "That's the idea."

"Do you have enough magic dust to make it across the lake?" Demetra asked.

"If I run out," Sabrina replied, "then I guess I'll have to swim."

Demetra covered her face and groaned, "Oh, no."

"I'll lead it near the Willow-that-Weeps," Sabrina said, thinking out loud. "Then maybe it will get caught in the Spinning Pool and disappear forever."

Suddenly the shadow beneath the water froze. It slowly turned. Two big yellow eyes rose to the surface of the lake.

It was looking straight up at Sabrina!

"Sabrina, I don't like your plan," Demetra said in a shaky voice. "Please get down from that window."

Sabrina's gaze was locked with the monster's. "I can't," she whispered. "It's watching me."

Very slowly Sabrina opened the purse at her waist. She carefully scooped up a handful of magic fairy dust. All the while she whispered instructions to her sisters.

"When I leave, you two go to the courtyard and guard my people," Sabrina murmured, barely moving her lips. "Tell them to stay on land. That's one place we know the monster won't go."

Suddenly the monster raised its head out of the water. Its big spiky teeth sparkled in the sunlight.

It's going to get me! Sabrina thought, nearly falling back into the room.

"She's fainting," Emily cried.

"No, I'm not." Sabrina squeezed her eyes closed and willed herself to be brave. She clutched the side of the windowsill with one hand and faced the monster.

"Sabrina, be sensible," Demetra pleaded. "You have to save yourself!"

"I will," Sabrina replied, as she flung the magic dust in the air. "But first I have to save my people."

5

Sparkle of Light

Sabrina looked down and smiled. Her plan was working. The monster was following her!

She flew close to the water so that the monster could see her. His big shadow mirrored her every move. If she turned, it turned. If she flew faster, it swam faster.

Across the lake Sabrina could see a patch of churning water by the Willow-that-Weeps. The Spinning Pool! She was about to head for it when something caught her eye.

A sparkle! A very golden sparkle.

Princess Sabrina shielded her eyes with her hand. The golden light was blinding. Where was it coming from?

Flash!

There it was again. Sabrina squinted toward the shore.

"My boat!" she cried. It was caught in the reeds by Bluebonnet Falls. "That golden light is coming from my boat!"

Inside the boat was the golden basket. It was glowing.

Suddenly Sabrina was being pulled out of the sky!

"What's happening to me?" she cried, as the light pulled her closer and closer to shore! "Stop!"

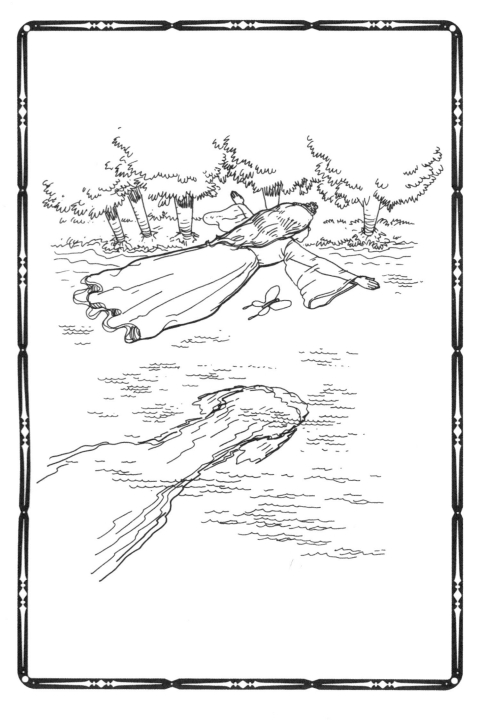

When she was just over the boat, the basket leaped into her hand. "My goodness!" she cried in surprise.

Sabrina gently landed on the grassy shore. For a moment she forgot all about the Blue Lake Monster. She thought only of the golden basket.

Sabrina knelt and placed the basket in front of her. Carefully she lifted the lid.

"Oh!"

There, tied with a sapphire blue ribbon, was the most beautiful pear the princess had ever seen. Its skin shimmered like polished gold.

She couldn't take her eyes off it.

Sabrina's mouth began to water. Her fingers twitched.

"I have to eat it," she murmured, picking up the pear.

Sabrina was about to take a juicy bite when she heard a huge splash in the lake.

"Nooooooo!" the monster roared, shooting out of the water. It towered above Sabrina's head. Then it opened its jaws and bent forward.

The princess froze with the pear in midair.

This is it, she thought, staring into the beast's mouth. *It's going to gobble me up.*

She shut her eyes and waited.

But she only felt a slight tug. At her fingers.

Sabrina opened her eyes and stared at her empty hand.

"My pear!" she gasped.

The Lake Monster had eaten it. The beast had swallowed the golden fruit in one gulp. And now something odd was happening to the monster.

Its gray skin turned green. Then it changed to a sickly yellow.

The monster swayed back and forth, its eyes rolling back in its head. Slowly, slowly, it fell forward.

"Ooomph!"

First the body hit the ground. Then the long neck stretched across the grass.

Finally the monster's head came to rest, with its nose in Princess Sabrina's lap.

6

The Poisoned Pear

Sabrina stared at the Lake Monster's head. It was as big as a boat. It lay with its eyes closed, breathing in shaky gusts of air through its nose.

Sabrina carefully reached up and touched the monster's nose. The yellow skin was soft, like the petals of a flower.

The monster sighed at her touch.

"Poor monster," Sabrina whispered. "You're sick."

The ragged breathing grew calmer. Sabrina's heart went out to this creature. It looked so sad and helpless.

"There's the princess!" a voice cried from behind her. "The monster has her in his clutches."

Sabrina turned to see her sisters rounding the bend by Bluebonnet Falls. They were leading many creatures from Blue Lake.

"Don't worry, Sabrina, we'll save you," Emily shouted, as she hiked up her skirt and raced to help the Sapphire Princess.

Zazz the Butterfly clung to the top of Emily's wild red hair and ordered, "Faster! Run faster!"

Gurt and several other Gilliwags hopped behind Emily and Zazz, waving wooden oars in the air.

"Save the Princess!" Gurt bellowed. "Kill the monster!"

"Stay back!" Sabrina cried, wrapping her arms around the monster's head. She pressed her cheek against its skin. She could hardly hear it breathe. "This creature is ill. Please, don't hurt it."

Princess Emily and the crowd stumbled to a stop. They were confused.

"But . . . but I don't understand," Emily stammered. "I thought that monster was trying to hurt you."

Sabrina looked at her sister with sad eyes. "That's what I thought, too. But I think it was only trying to help me."

Zazz fluttered above the golden basket that had fallen over on its side. The pears had tumbled onto the ground. Dead flies and ants lay around the golden fruit.

"Look, everyone!" Zazz cried. "This food . . . it was poisoned."

Demetra narrowed her eyes. "I knew something was wrong. That gift wasn't from a secret admirer."

"It was from a secret enemy," Emily finished.

"And it was *sooo* beautiful," Zazz murmured.

Sabrina stroked the monster's lumpy head. "You knew that pear was poisoned, didn't you? You ate it to save me."

Sabrina thought back to the first time the monster had bumped her boat. It

was when she touched the golden basket. Then the monster reared out of the water when Sabrina and Zazz were about to sneak a bite of chocolate.

"We were all wrong," Sabrina announced to her people. "This creature never tried to hurt me. Everything it did was to help me."

The monster moaned and rolled its head to one side.

Sabrina knew it was in great pain. Tears welled up in her eyes.

"You poor, dear creature," she said. "I wish there was something I could do to help you."

"Perhaps there is," a voice whispered across the wind.

Sabrina lifted her head and looked toward the lake. There, half-hidden in the reeds, was Sage.

"At the base of Bluebonnet Falls grows a tiny purple flower," the wisest of the Storkz said. "It has the power to heal." The monster groaned again and he added, "But you must be quick. There isn't much time."

Sabrina could have asked Gurt, or even Zazz, to go to the Falls. But this was one thing she had to do herself.

The monster had saved her life. Now she would return the favor.

7

The Spirit of Blue Lake

The purple flower grew only in one spot, directly behind the waterfall. To pick it, Sabrina had to dive through the rushing water.

Now the princess knelt before the dying monster. Her chiffon dress was soaked and clung to her body. Her blond hair hung dripping down her back. But she didn't care. Sabrina had the magic flower.

It took all her strength to pry open the monster's thick jaws. Finally she was able to place the flower on its tongue.

"Swallow this," she urged. "It will make you well."

Demetra and Emily stood with Zazz and the other Lake Dwellers at a safe distance. Even though the monster was ill, they still didn't trust it.

Sabrina stroked the monster's throat. "Please, try to swallow. I want you to live. You *have* to live."

After a few seconds, the creature swallowed.

"Good. You did it!" Sabrina cheered. "Now relax and let the flower work its magic."

Sabrina and her friends watched and waited. The cure seemed to take forever.

But ever so slowly, the sickly yellow skin turned back into a nice dark gray.

Sabrina kept petting the monster's head. Its breathing was becoming less harsh.

"That's a good monster," she cooed. "You're getting better. I can see it."

A low growl rattled the monster's throat. And all of the Lake Dwellers leaped back in alarm.

"Sabrina, be careful!" Demetra warned.

Sabrina ignored her sister and kept stroking the monster's nose and brow.

With each breath, it seemed to grow stronger. Soon its body began to twitch. Then its eyelids fluttered.

"It's waking up," Sabrina announced.

Demetra, Emily, and the others took another giant step backwards.

Sabrina held her breath.

At last the monster opened its eyes. It looked at Sabrina and big tears welled up in its yellow eyes.

"Please, don't look at me, Princess," the creature said in a sweet, lilting voice.

Sabrina blinked in surprise. The Lake Monster was a girl!

"I am too ugly," the monster said.

"But . . . but you're not ugly!" Sabrina cried. "You're beautiful."

The monster sighed. A deep sigh, full of sorrow. "There was a time when you might have said I was beautiful and everyone would have agreed with you." Her huge eyes narrowed. "That was before Lord Bleak and the Darklings ruled this land."

"You mean you haven't always looked like this?" Sabrina asked.

"Oh, no," the monster replied in her lovely voice. "I was once a mermaid with sea green eyes and skin the color of pearls. I was called Oona."

"Oona!" Zazz blurted. "I've heard stories of Oona."

Gurt nodded. "Oona is the Spirit of Blue Lake. They say she has been here since the beginning of time."

Oona nodded. "That I have. That I have."

"But why have we never seen or heard from you?" Sabrina asked.

Oona hung her head. "Because I am a monster," she said. "After Lord Bleak cast his spell on me, I tried to talk to my friends. But I scared them. They all ran from me."

"But we wouldn't run . . . ." Sabrina didn't finish her sentence. She realized that she *had* run from Oona. And so had her people. They all had been ready to destroy Oona just because of the way she looked.

"We made a mistake," Sabrina declared, looking at the crowd. "We thought just because the golden picnic basket was beautiful, it was good."

Zazz hung her head. "We were wrong."

Sabrina looked back at Oona. "And we thought just because you looked different from us, you were bad."

"And we were wrong again," Gurt added.

Sabrina knelt in front of the huge creature. Demetra, Emily, and the all the creatures of Blue Lake knelt, too.

"Dear Oona, will you accept our sincerest apology?" Sabrina asked.

The corners of Oona's gray lips curled into a smile. "Of course, my princess. And let me say that after years of hiding in the Deep Dark, at last I can say I am happy."

Everyone cheered. Sabrina stood up and clapped her hands in delight. "Oh, I wish we could celebrate this moment with a feast!"

Gurt stepped forward. "Princess, we still have the china and the tablecloths."

"And all of the guests are here," Zazz added.

"That's true. But we have no food to offer anyone." Sabrina pointed to the broken picnic basket and the poisoned food beside it. "Not one crumb."

Suddenly a shadow darkened the sky. It swooped over their heads with a rush of wind.

"Look out!" The Lake Dwellers clutched their heads and huddled in fear.

Sabrina looked up, frightened. But her fear soon turned to joy. She skipped over to her sisters and pointed skyward.

Emily laughed out loud. "Look who's here!"

Demetra opened one eye and peeked at the sky. "Well," she huffed. "It's about time!"

8

Four Crown Jewels

A great fire-breathing dragon circled
above the crowd. Riding on its back,
laughing and waving, was Roxanne, the
Ruby Princess.

Sabrina raced to greet her sister as
soon as the dragon touched down.
"You're here at last!"

Roxanne wore a ruby-red traveling
dress complete with red gloves and cape.
She tossed the cape over her shoulder
and hugged Sabrina. "It's so good to see
you! Did I miss anything?"

"Miss anything?" Demetra repeated, as she and Emily ran to join their sisters. "We've had an entire adventure while waiting for you."

Roxanne's dark eyes sparkled. "Oh, we love a good adventure." She turned to the green and red dragon. "Don't we, Hapgood?"

Hapgood was Roxanne's friend and palace advisor. He lived with the Ruby Princess in the Red Mountains.

The dragon nodded very formally to the princess. "My lady, life with you is one great adventure. I do enjoy it. It keeps me young."

Roxanne patted the dragon's neck. "That's the spirit, Happy."

Emily draped her arm around Sabrina's shoulder. "We're all together."

"Yes." Sabrina smiled fondly at her sisters. "Here we are, the four jewels of our kingdom."

Demetra nodded. "Now we have two reasons to celebrate. It's really too bad about our picnic, though."

"What happened?" Roxanne asked.

The other three looked at each other. Sabrina spoke first. "It's a very long story. Let me just say that our basket of food was poisoned."

"Who would have done such a thing?" Roxanne asked.

Demetra lowered her voice. "Lord Bleak and his Darklings."

"Oh!" Roxanne gasped, putting one gloved hand to her mouth. "Flying here we passed over the Mysterious Forest. Hapgood was certain he saw several Darklings running into the woods."

"They wore black capes and seemed terribly upset," Hapgood added.

"They were upset because their awful trick didn't work," Demetra cut in. "They tried to poison Sabrina."

"Luckily, Oona was there to save me," Sabrina declared.

"Oona?" Roxanne cocked her head. "Who is Oona?"

Sabrina pointed to the spot where the lake creature had been resting. It was empty.

"She was just over there by the shore, but she's gone," Sabrina said. "I hope she hasn't run away."

Emily leaned forward and whispered, "She's very shy, because of the way she looks."

"What does she look like?" Roxanne whispered back.

The three princesses paused, trying to find the words to describe the lake creature.

Before, Sabrina would have described Oona as gray and lumpy with fierce, pointed teeth. But now when she thought of Oona, she could only remember her eyes.

"She has big, golden eyes," Sabrina

said. "They are very warm and friendly. But there is also a touch of sadness in them. Her skin is like rose petals, soft and velvety."

"She's quite large," Demetra added. "Bigger than you, Hapgood. But that doesn't slow her down in the water."

Emily nodded. "She moves very fast and very gracefully through Blue Lake. She is afraid that she's ugly, but we think she's beautiful."

Sabrina was glad to see her sisters had changed their minds about the Blue Lake Monster. Now that they knew Oona, they admired and loved her, too.

Sabrina squinted out over the lake. "It's a shame we don't have any food. I was hoping Oona would join us for dinner."

"If it's food you need," Roxanne said, "I've got just the thing. Happy, show my sisters what we brought."

Hapgood unfolded one large red wing. Underneath were two huge picnic baskets.

"Happy packed us a wonderful lunch," Roxanne explained. "There's food enough for everyone."

Sabrina clapped her hands. "This is wonderful news! Zazz!" she called to the butterfly. "Hurry and tell everyone that our picnic celebration is about to begin. I have something I must do."

Zazz flew to the Gilliwags, who were

napping in the reeds. Then she zoomed to the Nymphs, who were frolicking in the pool at the base of Bluebonnet Falls. Then she hurried to find the Striders. They were skating near the shore of Blue Lake.

Gurt the Gilliwag spread a tablecloth on the grass and set out the royal china. Demetra, Emily, and Roxanne unpacked the picnic baskets.

While everyone prepared for their feast, Sabrina looked for Oona.

She found her in the murky waters near the Willow-that-Weeps. Oona clutched the golden basket in her mouth.

"What are you doing?" Sabrina

gasped. "Don't you remember? That basket is poisoned!"

Oona set the basket on a floating log. "I'm going to take this basket with its poisoned food to the bottom of our lake."

Sabrina's eyes widened. "Below the Deep Dark?"

Oona nodded. "I'm taking it to a place so deep that no creature will ever find it."

"But won't you join our picnic first?" Sabrina asked. "Roxanne brought an entire feast."

Oona smiled sadly. "I would love to join your feast. Maybe one day I will. But for now, I must do this. I want to make sure that Lord Bleak doesn't harm one more creature in our beautiful lake."

Sabrina stepped onto the floating log near the lake creature. She wrapped her arms around Oona's neck. "You have done so much to help us. Is there any way we can repay your kindness?"

Oona closed her eyes in thought. When she opened them again, she said, "I have been so lonely for so long. The best gift you could give me is your friendship."

"That you have," Sabrina promised. "And will always have."

With that, Oona scooped up the poisoned basket and plunged into the lake.

Sabrina stared at the ripple of water where Oona had just been.

And for one moment, Sabrina was certain she saw a beautiful mermaid with sea-green eyes and skin the color of pearls.

The Emerald Princess Plays a Trick

Table of Contents

Emily the Court Jester

Princess Emily slowly peeked around the trunk of the big elm tree. From where she hid, she could see Staghorn, the palace gardener. He was trimming the mulberry bushes that lined the path to her home in the Greenwood.

"Watch this," Emily whispered to her friend Arden, who stood a few feet behind her. "This is going to be *so* funny!"

Staghorn aimed his clippers at a small bush. Just as he snapped them shut,

Emily tugged on the string she was holding. The bush leaped away from the dwarf.

"Hey!" Staghorn cried, nearly falling backward. "What's going on?"

Emily covered her mouth. Her green eyes sparkled. Her red hair shook as she laughed.

Staghorn adjusted the glasses perched on the end of his nose. "My eyes must be playing tricks on me," he muttered.

He opened his clippers again, leaned toward the bush, and snapped the blades together.

Emily tugged on the string once more. The bush sprang in the air.

"Whoa!" Staghorn fell forward.

Emily burst out laughing.

"Hey!" Staghorn shouted, rubbing his nose. "What's so funny?"

Emily danced out from behind the tree.

Staghorn's face turned a bright red. "Princess Emily!" he cried, taking off his cap. "I didn't see you."

"Of course not, Staghorn," Emily giggled. She gave him a big hug. "I was hiding."

His furry eyebrows met in a frown. "Then it was *you* who made the bush hop away from me?"

"Yes!" Emily showed him the string she'd attached to the bush. "Wasn't that funny?"

Staghorn stared up at the Emerald

Princess for a long time. "Yes, Princess," he said finally. "It was very funny."

Emily pointed at him. "You should have seen the look on your face when the bush leaped in the air."

"I'm sure I looked very surprised," Staghorn said, brushing off the knees of his brown trousers.

"You looked positively silly!" Emily declared.

"I'm glad I made you laugh." Staghorn gestured down the path. "Now if you'll excuse me, Princess, I had better get on with my work. I have to do some pruning in the Twisted Vines."

Emily hugged the little man once more. "Thank you, my dear Staghorn.

You are a very good sport!"

She watched the dwarf hurry off into the trees. Then she turned to Arden. "Wasn't that fun?"

The beautiful white unicorn blinked her big brown eyes. "I think it may have been fun for you, Princess. But I'm not so sure about Mr. Staghorn."

"Oh, he loves tricks," Emily said, picking a tiny bluebell and braiding it into Arden's mane. "Staghorn is like a grandfather to me. I've been teasing him since I was a little girl at the Jewel Palace."

Emily and her three sisters grew up in the Jewel Palace. It sat at the heart of the Jewel Kingdom. Her parents, Queen

Jemma and King Regal, lived there.

"Did you see his face?" Arden asked.

Emily shrugged. "Staghorn always looks a little grumpy. That's why he's so much fun to play tricks on."

A bell chimed high above them. It came from the Emerald Palace, a magnificent tree house held up by six huge cedar trees.

On the tip of one of the pinecone-covered turrets sat a carved wooden clock. Emily had been given the clock by the people of the Greenwood when she was crowned the Emerald Princess.

Ding-ding-ding!

The clock chimed again.

"Did you hear that, Arden?" Emily asked. "It must be noon."

Arden turned her head. "Weren't you supposed to meet Princess Roxanne now?"

Emily's big green eyes widened. She covered her mouth with her hand. "I almost forgot! We're supposed to meet at the edge of the Greenwood."

Princess Roxanne was the Ruby Princess and she lived high in the Red Mountains. Roxanne had been visiting Demetra, the Diamond Princess. Demetra was the oldest sister. She ruled the White Winterland.

"Arden, would you mind giving me a ride?" the Emerald Princess asked the unicorn. "We'll reach the border much quicker that way."

"Hop on, Princess." Arden ducked her head and bent one knee.

Emily hiked up her green velvet skirt and hopped onto the unicorn's back.

"I have a special surprise for my sister." Princess Emily patted the small package she held in her lap. "But I need to be at the border before Princess Roxanne."

"Surprise?" Arden asked, as she cantered beneath the rustling leaves of the Greenwood. "What is it?"

Emily bent close to the unicorn's ear and whispered, "If I told you, it wouldn't be a surprise." She patted her friend's neck. "Now let's hurry, please!"

Arden broke into a gallop. She leaped

lightly over a fallen log, then ducked under a low-hanging branch.

Emily threw her head back and flung her arms out to the sides. "What a wonderful day!"

Ahead, they could see bright light, where the Greenwood ended and the Rushing River began.

"Head for that big gray rock by the river," Emily cried, as they burst out of the woods.

"What are we going to do there?" Arden asked.

"Not *we*," Emily said, hopping off Arden's back. "Me."

The Princess unwrapped the bundle she'd been carrying and pulled out a black hooded cape. "Keep a lookout for Princess Roxanne, will you?"

The unicorn looked toward a dark line of trees cutting across the meadow. "I think I see her," Arden announced. "Coming out of the Mysterious Forest."

"Perfect." Emily slipped the hooded cape over her head. She darted behind the big rock. "Now hide yourself, Arden. I'm going to give my sister the surprise of her life."

"But my lady . . ." Arden started to say.

Emily put one finger to her lips and pointed towards rock across the clearing. Arden obediently trotted out of sight.

The Ruby Princess was hard to miss.

Roxanne wore a red satin dress that flashed in the afternoon sun. A crown with one gleaming ruby rested on top of her jet-black hair. And on her arm she wore a bright red-and-silver shield.

Roxanne paused on the bank of the Rushing River and squinted toward the Greenwood.

"Not yet," Emily whispered to herself. "Wait. Wait . . . ."

Roxanne hopped across the Rushing River, following a path of smooth gray stones.

"Here she comes," Emily giggled.

Roxanne stopped to squeeze the water out of the hem of her dress.

"Almost." Emily bent her knees.

Roxanne took two steps forward.

Emily raised her hands above her head.

Roxanne turned.

Emily shouted.

"*Boo!*"

2

Roxanne Sees Red

"You scared me!" Princess Roxanne cried, once she realized it was Emily hiding beneath the cape.

"I know!" Tears of laughter rolled down Emily's cheeks. "You screamed so loudly, you nearly scared me!"

Roxanne usually enjoyed a good joke. But this was not funny. Her dark eyes flashed and she stomped one foot. "Emily, stop laughing this instant!"

That only made Emily laugh harder.

"I was truly frightened," the Ruby

Princess went on. "I thought you were a Darkling."

Emily slapped her knee. "Isn't that funny?"

"There is nothing funny about Darklings," Roxanne said, glaring at her sister. "They are our worst enemies."

The Darklings and their ruler, Lord Bleak, had been banished from the Jewel Kingdom years before. They now lived far across the Black Sea.

"It is a terrible sign when a Darkling appears in our land," Roxanne continued. "As a princess of the Jewel Kingdom you should understand that."

"I do," Emily said, as she wiped the tears from her cheeks. "But we can't worry about them all the time. We should be able to have some fun."

"Scaring people is not my idea of fun," Roxanne declared.

"Oh, come on!" Emily swatted playfully at her sister's shoulder. "Don't be a stick-in-the-mud. I play tricks on my friends in the Greenwood all the time. They love it."

Roxanne arched an eyebrow. "Are you sure?"

"Of course. Ask Arden." Emily pointed to the unicorn, who stepped out from behind the other rock. "She'll tell you."

"Arden!" Roxanne cried happily. "I'm so glad you're here."

The unicorn bowed low. "Hello,

Princess Roxanne. It's a pleasure to see you."

"My sister and I are having a discussion," Roxanne explained. "She says the tricks she plays on everyone are funny. What do you think, Arden?"

Arden ducked her head and studied a small circle of pansies at her feet. "Well . . ."

"Be honest!" Roxanne advised.

"I think practical jokes are only funny to the people who play them," Arden finally said.

Roxanne put her hands on her hips and faced Emily. "See?"

Emily waved one hand. "That's just Arden. She's too sensitive."

Arden blinked her eyes patiently.

Emily hopped onto a moss-covered log and carefully walked the entire length of it. "Tell me, sister, why are you in such a bad mood today?"

"You put me in a bad mood," Roxanne replied.

"Oh, fiddle!" Emily spun. "You know, I *had* planned a fun afternoon for us."

"Doing what?" Roxanne asked.

"First we *were* going to visit the fairies. They're making a cradle out of a walnut shell for Ivy's new baby."

"The baby has lavender eyes," Arden told Roxanne. "She's a beautiful fairy child."

Emily perched on a thick root. "Then we *were* going to have dewberry tea at the Emerald Palace. And after that, we *were* going for a swim at Looking-glass Pond."

"*Were?*" Roxanne repeated.

Emily sighed dramatically and tilted her nose up to the sky. "Now I'm not sure we should do any of those things. You are being such a grump."

"Grump!" Roxanne's jaw dropped open. "Emily, that's a mean thing to say."

Emily shrugged. "I'm just being honest."

"No," Roxanne replied. "You're being impossible!"

Emily nearly fell off her log. "What?"

"And selfish!" Roxanne marched up to the log and put her face close to Emily's.

"And I don't feel like spending another second with you!"

With a brisk nod to Arden, Roxanne turned and marched out of the forest.

"Roxanne!" Emily cried, trying to get her balance. "Where are you going?"

"To Blue Lake," Roxanne shouted over her shoulder. "To see Sabrina. I'm sure *she'll* be happy to see me."

Sabrina, the Sapphire Princess, was the fourth Jewel Princess. She lived across from the Greenwood in Blue Lake.

"Roxanne, please wait!" Emily leaped off the log and ran to follow her sister. "I was just kidding. I'm happy to see you. Come back!"

Princess Roxanne didn't even turn

around. She marched straight across the Rushing River and kept going until she reached the edge of the Mysterious Forest. Then she turned and looked back at Emily and Arden.

"What's she doing?" Emily murmured.

Roxanne slowly raised the red-and-silver shield fastened to her right arm. She murmured a few words and vanished.

"Did you see that!" Emily gasped to Arden. "Roxanne used her magic shield so I wouldn't be able to see her. Why would she do—?"

"Princess!" a new voice called.

Emily spun and watched as a young man stumbled out of the Greenwood. He wore a leather vest and feathered cap.

It was Crosscut, the young woodsman.

"Princess," Crosscut gasped, falling to one knee. "Come quickly. Staghorn is hurt."

"Staghorn the gardener?" Emily repeated. "But I just saw him a short while ago. He said he was off to prune the Twisted Vines."

"Something went wrong," Crosscut explained. "He got caught in the Twisted Vines and now he's in great pain. Please come quickly."

This was very serious.

"Thank you for telling me, Crosscut," Emily declared. "We'll go to him at once."

3

Staghorn Is Hurt!

When they reached the Twisted Vines,
Crosscut took Princess Emily and Arden
to Staghorn. He was lying on his back
beside the Babbling Brook. A fairy
named Hazelnut was tending to his leg.

"Staghorn!" Emily cried, kneeling
beside the little dwarf. "Where are you
hurt?"

Staghorn turned his head away.

"It's his ankle," Hazelnut replied. "I
think it's broken."

"Oh, dear!" Emily stood up. "We

must get him to the Emerald Palace."

"No!" Staghorn cried out. "Not the palace. I want to go to see Nana Woodbine."

Nana was famous all over the Greenwood for her healing powers. She lived in a tiny cottage at the Heart-o'-the-Wood. Her mother had been half fairy, half wood sprite, and her father was a wizard.

"Nana is the perfect person to call," Emily told Hazelnut. "Let's bring Staghorn to my palace, and we'll send for Nana Woodbine."

"No!" Staghorn cried again. "I don't want to go to the Palace."

"Go to Nana Woodbine's," Hazelnut

said, fluttering above Staghorn's head. "You'll be safe there."

"Please, help me up!" Staghorn said, gesturing to Crosscut, the young woodsman.

Emily bent to help, but Staghorn shook her off. Crosscut gave the Princess an apologetic shrug and helped Staghorn to his feet.

"How did Staghorn get hurt?" Emily asked Hazelnut, as Crosscut and the dwarf hobbled away from them.

"Why do I need to tell you?" Hazelnut said rudely. Her wings buzzed as she hovered above Emily.

Arden pranced forward. "Because she is Princess of the Greenwood, and she has asked you a question."

Hazelnut scowled. Then she perched on a nearby limb and pointed across the brook. A rope dangled from the limb of a sycamore tree. "That rope caught Staghorn by the ankle and yanked him up to the treetops. Luckily the woodsman was here to cut him down."

"Poor Staghorn!" Emily gasped. "He could have hung there for a very long time!"

"But where did the rope come from?" Arden asked.

"Ask the princess," Hazelnut said, as she flew away. "*She* should know."

Emily was confused. No one in her kingdom had ever spoken to her that

way before. She turned to Arden and asked, "What did Hazelnut mean by that?"

Arden touched Emily's shoulder with her horn. "Don't let her worry you, Princess," the unicorn murmured. "Staghorn is the one who needs your concern. Let us go to Nana Woodbine and see if there is anything we can do to help the poor man."

"As always, you are right," Emily said, smiling at her friend. "Let's not waste another second."

4

Hurry to Nana Woodbine

Nana Woodbine's cottage was covered in ivy. Bright-red shutters framed the windows. Cheery clouds of smoke puffed out of the stone chimney.

Emily raised her hand to ring the bell. But before she could touch it, the door swung open.

"Welcome, Princess," Nana Woodbine said with a sweet smile. "I knew you would come."

Nana was beautiful. She had delicate features and eyes the color of the ocean.

Tiny flowers were woven into the braids circling the top of her head.

Emily peeked around Nana. She could see Staghorn lying on a carved wooden bed in front of the fire. He was surrounded by his Greenwood friends.

"How is Staghorn's ankle?" Emily asked.

"It isn't broken," Nana replied.

Emily heaved a sigh of relief. "Oh, thank goodness."

"But it is very badly bruised." Nana Woodbine whispered, "And so is Staghorn's pride. He felt like a fool hanging upside down like that."

Emily nodded. "I would have, too. May I see him?"

Nana frowned. "I don't think that's a very good idea. He needs to rest."

"But isn't there something I can do to help?" Emily asked.

"No, Princess," Nana replied. "I've rubbed his ankle with sneezewort and I'm about to give him a spoonful of mercury vine. Now if you'll excuse me . . ."

Before Emily could say another word, Nana closed the door in her face.

Emily turned to Arden. "Something very odd is going on here. Why wouldn't Nana let me talk to Staghorn?"

"I don't know, Princess," the unicorn replied. "But it is very strange."

Laughter erupted inside.

"I wish I were a tiny mouse," Emily

said, "so I could creep inside that cottage and hear what they're all saying."

"Why don't you use your magic pan flute?" the unicorn suggested. "The one that the great wizard Gallivant gave you."

Emily's eyes widened. "My pan flute! But I've never used it before."

Arden smiled. "There's always a first time."

Emily wore the pan flute on a golden rope draped over one shoulder. "The high note will make me small," she said, remembering what the wizard had told her. "And the low note will make me tall."

Arden nodded. "That's right, my princess. But remember, once you are

small, you must stay that way until sundown."

"I remember." Emily touched the flute and felt a tingle in her fingertips.

"Are you ready?" Arden asked.

"I think so." Emily carefully raised the pipes to her lips. "Here goes."

The princess took a deep breath and blew the highest note possible.

There was a flash of light, and a loud whirring sound filled the air.

One second later, Emily found herself standing beneath a large mushroom. She was staring into the pink eyes of a little gray mouse.

Princess Emily and the mouse were exactly the same size!

5

Teeny Tiny Princess

"Shoo!" Emily shouted in the mouse's face. "Get away from me."

The mouse twitched his whiskers several times, then bared his teeth.

That made Emily very nervous. She grabbed a twig lying near the mushroom and waved it at the mouse.

"Go back to your home or I'll . . . I'll bop you on the nose!" Emily cried.

The mouse curled his lips, but after a few seconds, he scampered away.

"Phew!" Emily said, collapsing against

the stem of the mushroom. "That was close."

Suddenly a big white furry thing loomed in front of Emily's face.

"Good heavens!" The princess instantly squeezed her eyes closed and covered her head. "It's going to get me!"

But all she felt was a gust of warm wind.

Emily cracked one eye open, then tilted her head back. The white furry thing was Arden's nose. And the warm wind was coming from the unicorn's nostrils!

"Princess?" Arden's voice boomed in Emily's ears. "Are you all right?"

Emily covered her ears and shouted

back, "I'm fine, but it's a little scary to be so small. Even the tiniest mouse could hurt me."

"Why don't you let me pick you up with my teeth and carry you to Nana's front door?" Arden suggested.

Emily looked at the unicorn's huge ivory teeth and gulped. One mistake and Arden could nip her in two!

"Don't worry," Arden whispered. "I'll be very, very careful. I'll only bite your dress."

Emily knew she had to trust her friend. "All right, Arden." She turned her back so the unicorn could grab hold of her skirt. "Lift me up!"

Arden carefully bit down on the

emerald green dress. Then she gently lifted the princess into the air.

"Whee!" Emily giggled, watching the ground zoom away from her. "I feel like I'm flying."

Arden walked ever so slowly up the stone steps to Nana Woodbine's front door and set Emily down.

"That was fun!" Emily giggled. "It was just like being at the tiptop of the Greenwood."

"I'll wait for you here," Arden said.

Emily saluted the unicorn, then knelt down and peered beneath Nana's door. There was just enough room for her to squeeze under it.

She crossed her fingers. "I just hope

no one steps on me when I get inside."

Emily flattened herself against the top step and wiggled her way into Nana's cottage. It was snug and warm and smelled of freshly baked bread.

"Mmmmm! Delicious!" Emily murmured, as she straightened up. She tried to find Staghorn, but a pair of old worn boots blocked her view of the room.

Emily recognized the boots.

"Why, it's Fluke, the fisherman!" she said, stepping backwards and looking up at the gray-bearded old man. "Word certainly travels fast!"

Fluke tended the Greenwood's brooks and streams. He and Staghorn were great friends. He must have run to Nana's when he heard that Staghorn was hurt.

"I'll hide under the bed where Staghorn is resting," Emily murmured, inching her way along the wall. "That way I can see and hear everything."

Fluke, Hazelnut, and Crosscut circled the bed. They were listening to Staghorn tell a story about his old days at the Jewel Palace.

"Queen Jemma and King Regal always treated me like one of the family," Staghorn was saying. "There was many a time that I pulled all four of the Jewel Princesses around that garden in their little rainbow-colored wagon."

Emily couldn't help smiling. Those

were fun times for her, too. She scurried under the bed, anxious to hear more.

"It would break King Regal's heart if he heard how the Emerald Princess was treating the people of the Greenwood," Staghorn said.

"What!" Emily gasped from her hiding spot behind the bed leg.

Hazelnut fluttered onto the quilt and squeaked, "Just yesterday the princess nearly scared the stuffing out of the palace cook. Mrs. Dumpling's hands shook so much she completely ruined the cake she'd spent three hours decorating."

Emily winced. She had no idea Mrs. Dumpling was so upset.

Nana Woodbine sat on the edge of

the bed. "I know this mercury vine tastes terrible," she told Staghorn, nodding at the wooden spoon in her hand. "But I want you to swallow it before you tell any more stories."

"Give it to Princess Emily!" Fluke joked. "It would serve her right."

The group burst into laughter.

Emily could feel her cheeks turn a bright red. Her friends were making fun of her!

"I'll bet the Princess has played a trick on everyone in the Greenwood!" Fluke declared. "She's played at least three on me."

" And this is the worst part," Hazelnut added. "We all have to pretend her jokes are funny, just because she's our princess!"

Emily shook her head. "Oh, no."

"I'm going to speak to King Regal about this," Fluke said, slamming his fist in his hand. "When a princess starts hurting her own people, then it's time for her to stop being a princess."

"They think I'm the one who trapped Staghorn!" Emily gasped.

Emily's chin started to quiver and hot tears welled up in her eyes. *I have to get out of here*, she thought. *I have to run.*

Emily stumbled out from under the bed and headed straight for the cottage door. She didn't care if anyone saw her or even stepped on her.

Arden was waiting for the princess when she rolled out from under Nana's door.

"Oh, Arden, I'm so ashamed," Emily cried, burying her face in her hands. "You and Roxanne were right. No one liked my tricks. They only pretended that they did. Now they're all blaming me for Staghorn's injury."

"But you had nothing to do with it," Arden replied.

"You know it and I know it, but how do we convince them?" Emily whimpered. "They think I'm a terrible princess."

"If only we knew who *really* set that trap," Arden murmured. "Then you could straighten things out with Staghorn."

Emily's green eyes grew wide. "That's it! All I have to do is find out who did it!"

"I'll help you!" Arden declared.

Emily smiled at Arden, swiping at her tears with the back of her hand. "Thank you, my friend. I'll be forever grateful." Then she straightened up to her full six-inch height. "We had better get straight to it. Time's a-wasting."

Arden bowed. "Just tell me what to do, Princess."

Emily climbed down the stone steps of Nana's cottage. "I want you to take a message to Princess Roxanne. She's at

Blue Lake. Ask her to join me as soon as possible."

"But where are you going?" Arden asked.

Emily raced through the tall blades of glass, slashing at them with a twig. "Back to the scene of the crime," she cried. "You'll find me at the Twisted Vines!"

Back to the Twisted Vines

Emily bent over to catch her breath. It had taken her two hours to run to the Twisted Vines.

"If I weren't so small I would have been here ages ago!" she huffed, clutching her side. "Now I'm tired and very hungry."

She spied a blackberry bush on the path in front of her. Emily stood on tiptoe and reached for a big, ripe berry. But something blocked her way.

At first she thought it was just a

spider's web covered in leaves and twigs.

Emily poked at the web. It was strong, like rope.

"Wait a minute," she murmured. "This isn't a spider's web. It's a net! But what is it doing here?"

Emily carefully lifted a blackberry leaf and peered through the netting. Underneath the net was a big wooden cage.

"The trap is set!" a voice rasped above her.

Emily spun and nearly fainted. She was staring directly at the biggest, ugliest feet she had ever seen. They were bony knobs with big tufts of fur on the toes and heels.

Slowly Emily raised her head. The feet belonged to two creatures in long black capes and hoods. She couldn't see their faces, but she knew who they were.

"Darklings!" she murmured. "I can't let them see me!"

Luckily Emily was wearing green. She backed up against the leaves stuck to the netting, hoping to blend in.

"This cage will hold one very stout dwarf and maybe a few of his fairy friends," the other Darkling said in a crackly voice.

"That's good," the first one replied. "If we capture them two and three at a time, our plan will move much faster."

"Plan?" Emily gulped.

"These Greenwood folk will make good workers for Lord Bleak."

Emily's hands flew to her face. These awful Darklings were planning to kidnap her people. She had to stop them!

"But how can I do that?" Emily looked down at herself. "I'm just one person, and a tiny person at that."

Keeping close to the ground, Emily bolted through the grass to a hickory tree at the edge of the Twisted Vines. There she scurried up the trunk and hid in the crook of the first branch.

Below her the Darklings had finished setting their trap.

"I've got to warn my people!" Emily declared, as she watched the caped figures hurry off to hide in the forest. "I need to find a Shinnybin."

The fastest way to get a message to anyone who lived in the Greenwood was to use a Shinnybin. They were sweet-faced creatures with long arms and legs.

A Shinnybin could climb to the top of a tree in a matter of seconds. Once there, he or she used a system of clicks and knocks to spread the news through the forest.

Emily, who still had her twig, carefully tapped on the bark of the birch tree. Two slow knocks, three quick, and a whistle.

She was immediately answered by a *rat-a-tat!*, a whistle, and a shriek of delight, as a furry creature swung onto her limb.

It was the Shinnybin named Sorrel.

She blinked several times at the princess, but asked no questions.

"At your service," Sorrel finally said. "What can I do for you?"

Emily wanted to tell Sorrel that two of Lord Bleak's Darklings had set the trap that hurt Staghorn. But she was afraid Sorrel wouldn't believe her.

"Please deliver this message to my people," Emily finally said. "The Twisted Vines are dangerous. Stay away! What happened to Staghorn could happen to you!"

Sorrel flopped her long arm across her

brow in a salute. "Got it! I'm on my way, Princess."

Suddenly the Shinnybin sprang to the next tree and shinnied to the top. Within seconds, Emily could hear the clicks and knocks of her message being sent across the treetops.

Princess Emily was about to follow the Darklings to their hiding place when she heard a voice singing below her.

"Me name is Fluke and me game is fish, Ta-roll, ta-roddle, ta-rish!"

"Fluke!" Emily gasped. "He's headed right for the Darkling trap!" She cupped her hands around her mouth and screamed, "Fluke! Look out!"

Fluke stopped walking and scratched his ear. "Eh?"

"Oh, dear," Emily murmured. "I'm too little for him to hear me." She climbed down the trunk of the tree until she was eye level with the fisherman.

"Fluke, look at the tree! It's me, Emily!"

The old fisherman turned his head. When he saw the tiny princess, he leaped backwards. "Hey, what's going on here? Is that you, Princess?"

Emily shouted as loudly as she could. "Yes, it's me!"

Fluke leaned his face towards her. "But how did you—?"

Emily waved one hand. "Never mind about that! You're in danger. Don't go into the Twisted Vines."

A cloud covered the old man's face. "Is this another one of your tricks?"

"No!" Emily placed one hand on her heart. "I swear it!"

Fluke narrowed his eyes. "I don't believe you, Princess. I'm off to find an herb for Nana Woodbine. And I have to follow that path!"

He pointed at where the cage was hidden.

"No, please!" Emily cried. "It's a trap!"

"Sorry, Princess," Fluke replied. Then he swung his pack over one shoulder and marched toward the cage.

The princess didn't hesitate. She

hurled herself through the air, landing on Fluke's shoulder.

"I can't let them catch you!" Emily declared, as the fisherman neared the trap. "They'll have to take me first!"

With a great heave, Emily leaped off his shoulder and flung herself at the netting.

Snap! The netting tightened around her.

Thunk! Emily dropped into the cage.

Whoosh! The cage, with Princess Emily trapped inside, was yanked up to the treetops!

7

Trapped!

As Princess Emily swung back and forth
in the treetops, Fluke looked up at her
in dismay.

"Are you all right?" he shouted.

Emily pressed her face against the cage
and called, "I'm a little bruised, but
fine."

"Please forgive me, Princess!" the
fisherman cried, clutching his hat to his
chest. "I thought you were just playing
another trick."

"Don't worry about that, Fluke!"

Princess Emily shouted down to the poor fisherman. "We haven't time."

She knew the Darklings weren't far away. If she and Fluke didn't do something quickly, they both would be taken prisoner.

"Cut me down!" She pointed at the rope tied to her cage. "Hurry!"

Fluke reached for the knife on his belt and ran for the rope. It was wrapped around a big wooden stake in the ground.

While Fluke sawed at the rope, Emily kept a lookout for Darklings. It was getting late and the sky had turned a pinkish color, which made it harder to see.

"Princess Emily!" Fluke called from

below. "My knife can't cut this rope! It's too thick!"

"Oh, no!" Emily could see the Darklings making their way through the trees.

"Forget about the rope," she cried. "Hide yourself."

"But what about you?" Fluke asked.

Emily looked at the setting sun and had an idea.

If the Darklings walked slowly, she might be able to save Fluke and herself.

"I have a plan," she cried to Fluke. "Now go hide!"

Fluke ducked into the bushes several yards from the trap, while Emily stared at the sun. She held her breath, watching

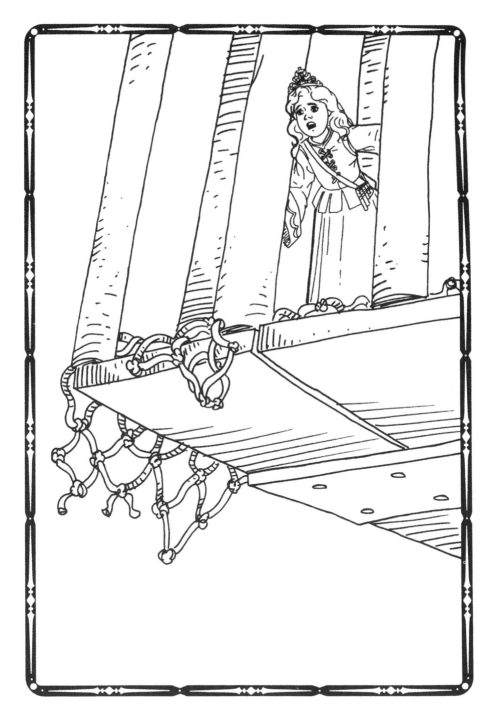

it slip slowly toward the horizon.

"Only a few minutes more," she whispered.

Unfortunately, at that moment, Emily heard another set of voices. Familiar voices. Coming from the direction of the Babbling Brook.

She ran to the other side of the cage. "Roxanne!" she gasped. "And Arden!"

They were heading straight for the Twisted Vines. And the Darklings!

"Sister! Stop!" Emily shouted at the Ruby Princess, but her tiny voice couldn't be heard over the rush of the brook.

Emily darted to the other side of the cage. The Darklings were moving more swiftly now.

This was terrible! What if they captured Roxanne? Then Lord Bleak would have both the Emerald Princess and the Ruby Princess in his clutches!

Emily felt for the pan flute at her waist as she looked back at the sun. "Hurry up and set!" she ordered.

Crack! A twig snapped just below her. The first Darkling had arrived at the trap.

He looked up at the cage and cackled. "Well, what have we here? It looks like we've caught ourselves a tiny . . ."

His voice caught in his throat as he realized his prisoner wasn't one of the fairy folk, but a real princess.

"The Emerald Princess!" the other

Darkling gasped when he arrived. "But how did she get so small?"

Emily could feel her knees grow weak. They'd caught her and soon they would catch her sister. She looked back at the sun.

"Lower the cage," the first one ordered. "Let's have a look at her."

The cage jerked toward the Darklings. But Emily never took her eyes off the sun.

The cage hit the ground with a thud. Emily reached one shaking hand toward her flute.

Arden and the Ruby Princess stepped out of the woods. "What have you done to my sister!" Roxanne cried.

The two Darklings turned, just as the sun disappeared below the horizon.

"This is our lucky day!" one shouted.

But then Emily raised the flute to her lips . . . and blew!

The Last Laugh

Bits of wood shot everywhere as Princess Emily burst out of the cage.

In an instant she turned from a six-inch princess into a giant as tall as a tree.

The Darklings screamed in fright. They turned to run.

"Not so fast!" Emily's voice boomed.

She grabbed the Darklings by their hoods and lifted them over Roxanne and Arden. They dangled high in the air.

"Please don't hurt us!" the first one begged.

"I want you to leave my land, do you hear?" she roared.

"Yes, Princess," the second one cried. "Please just put us down."

Emily held them over a thorn bush. "Promise me you'll never come back."

"We promise!" the Darklings moaned.

"And if I ever catch you in the Jewel Kingdom again," she warned, lifting them higher in the air, "I'll turn you into teeny, tiny bugs."

"No!" the Darklings howled.

Emily dropped them beside the Babbling Brook. The Darklings leaped across the stream and fled without ever looking back.

"Well, I guess we've seen the last of

those two," Emily declared to Arden and her sister.

Roxanne had been speechless since Emily turned into a giant. Finally she gasped, "Emily, you were magnificent!"

Emily bowed. "Thank you, sister."

"Can you really turn people into bugs?" Fluke called from his hiding place behind a hollow stump.

Emily laughed so hard her breath shook the tree branches. "Of course not. But they don't know that."

Roxanne stood on tiptoe and called, "What's the view like up there?"

"I can see everything," Emily replied. "The Emerald Palace, Nana Woodbine's cottage. Why, I think I've even spotted another one of those awful Darkling traps."

She leaned toward a red cedar growing almost ten feet away. Emily carefully tugged on something that looked like a vine. In an instant the trap sprang. Another cage just like the one that had caught her flew into the air.

"We must be sure to warn our people about these," Emily told Arden. "There could be more that I don't see."

Arden bowed. "Yes, Princess."

"Excuse me, Princess," Fluke said, inching forward. "I'd like to thank you for saving my life."

Emily touched the old man on the head with her fingertip. "It was nothing,

Fluke. I would have done the same for anyone in my kingdom. I just wish they knew that."

"Don't worry, Princess," Sorrel the Shinnybin cried, as she swung from her treetop to join the group. "I'll spread the word."

"And I will, too," Fluke added. "Sorrel and I will see to it that Staghorn and Nana Woodbine know who really set those traps. And who saved my life."

"Thank you both," Emily said with a smile. "I owe everyone in the Greenwood an apology, but first I must speak to my sister."

Emily knelt, so she could speak to Roxanne privately. "I've learned that my tricks only hurt people's feelings," Emily confessed. "And I want to apologize for scaring you today."

Roxanne grinned up at her sister. "Apology accepted."

Emily raised her right hand. "I won't ever do it again."

"That's the best news I've heard all day," Roxanne replied.

Emily stood up and clapped her hands. "Now what do you say we all go to my palace and celebrate?"

"And what's the special occasion?" Fluke asked.

"The end of Princess Emily's practical jokes," Roxanne declared.

"I'll celebrate that!" Arden cried.

Princess Roxanne tapped her sister's knee. "Emily, I'm getting a crick in my neck. Do you think you could change back now?"

Arden cleared her throat nervously. "Um . . . she can't."

"I can't?" Emily gasped. "Why not?"

"Once you've used your magic flute to change size, you must remain that way for another half turn around the sun," Arden explained.

"You mean I have to stay this way until morning?" Emily cried.

Arden nodded.

This tickled Roxanne so much she nearly fell over laughing.

"What's so funny?" Emily demanded.

"For once, dear sister," Roxanne giggled, "the joke is on you!"

Little by little, Princess Emily's frown changed into a smile. Soon she was giggling as hard as her friends. And the Greenwood rang with their laughter.

The Diamond Princess Saves the Day

Table of Contents

1

On the Ice

"Put on your skates and follow me," Demetra called to her sister. "Hurry!"

The Diamond Princess was dressed in her favorite white velvet skating skirt and jacket. She slipped on her silver skates and leaped lightly onto the crystal pond. Then she skated as fast as she could toward the center of the ice, her long brown braid flying behind her.

"Demetra, don't skate so fast," Sabrina shouted after her. "You're much better at this than I am. We don't do any skating where I live."

Sabrina was the Sapphire Princess. She lived in her palace at the Blue Lake. It was a watery world of weeping willows and lily pads.

This was the total opposite of Demetra's kingdom. Her palace sat in the heart of the White Winterland, a world of ice and snow.

"I have something very important to ask you." Demetra spun around to face Sabrina. "But I don't want any of my people to hear."

"Is it about the Winterfest?" Sabrina asked.

The Winterfest, which would begin

that evening, was one of the biggest events in the White Winterland. The festival was three wonderful days filled with music, dance, and feasts.

"The Winterfest is fine." Demetra said. "It's Finley who's the problem."

Finley was a fluffy white fox who held the important job of being Demetra's palace advisor.

"What's happened?" Sabrina asked, catching hold of her sister's arm. "Did you two have a fight?"

Demetra sighed, "All we do is fight!"

"Oh, Demetra, that's terrible," Sabrina said. "How long has this been going on?"

"Practically since the day I was

crowned the Diamond Princess," Demetra replied. "But it's gotten much worse since we began planning the Winterfest."

"What do you fight about?" Sabrina asked.

"Everything," Demetra said, throwing her hands in the air. "This morning we fought over who would judge the ice sculptures. And this afternoon we argued over where we would serve the hot cider and cookies after the ice show."

Sabrina tapped her chin with one mittened hand. "I don't like the sound of this."

"Me either." Demetra folded her arms across her chest. "I thought Finley was supposed to be my friend."

"He is," Sabrina replied. "Just like Zazz the butterfly is my friend and advisor."

Demetra nodded. "And Hapgood the Dragon is Roxanne's friend and advisor."

"And Arden the Unicorn is Emily's," Sabrina added.

Roxanne and Emily were their sisters, the Ruby and Emerald Princesses. They had all grown up at the Jewel Palace until King Regal and Queen Jemma gave them each their own kingdom to rule. Roxanne was given the Red Mountains and Emily reigned over the Greenwood.

"Then what's the matter with Finley?" Demetra asked.

"Maybe the problem isn't just Finley," Sabrina said, pursing her lips. "Maybe it's you."

Demetra cocked her head. "Me?"

Sabrina nodded. "Sometimes you can be a teensy bit bossy!"

"Bossy!" Demetra gasped.

"When we were growing up," Sabrina continued, "you used to order Roxanne and Emily around all the time. And they didn't like it one bit."

Demetra dug at the ice with the toe of her skate but said nothing.

"Remember, you have to be a friend to have one," Sabrina reminded her.

"Well, maybe I am a little bossy," Demetra finally confessed. "But so is

Finley. He thinks he knows everything about the Winterfest."

"Finley probably does know a lot," Sabrina pointed out. "He grew up here. And this is your first Winterfest."

"But that doesn't give him the right to call me names," Demetra protested. "This morning he said I was just a pigheaded princess!"

"What!" Sabrina exclaimed in surprise. "That's not a very nice thing to say."

"Princess Demetra!" a familiar voice shouted from behind them. It surprised Demetra so much she nearly fell down.

"Finley!" Demetra gasped when she turned around. The white fox was standing on the ice behind her.

As upset as she was with Finley, Demetra didn't want him to know she'd been talking about him. "How long have you been there?"

"I only just got here," Finley replied, stiffly. "I have a message to deliver."

Demetra responded in the same stiff way. "What is your message?"

"There seems to be a problem at Sparkle Mountain." Finley pointed to the sky in the west. An odd greenish cloud formed a circle around the tallest peak.

Demetra had never seen anything like it before. She forgot all about being angry with Finley and concentrated on her job as princess.

"This is most unusual," she declared. "I had better go see what's the matter."

Finley nodded. "I've already arranged for a sleigh to take you to Sparkle Mountain."

The tinkling of harness bells rang in the crisp air as Rolf the reindeer pulled the crystal sleigh up beside them.

"Sabrina, will you oversee the rest of the Winterfest preparations?" Demetra asked.

Sabrina nodded. "You can count on me."

Demetra hurried to the crystal sleigh, but Finley hopped in ahead of her.

"I'm coming with you," the fox said.

Demetra put her hands on her hips.

"I'm sorry, Finley, but you have to stay here. Sabrina needs your help."

"You're the one who needs my help," Finley said. "The road to Sparkle Mountain is very tricky."

Demetra flipped her braid over one shoulder. "I'm sure Rolf and I can figure it out. Now, please get out of the sleigh."

Finley shook his head stubbornly. "You won't be able to find the path up the mountain. It's hidden. I'm the one who knows how to find it."

"I think you should take Finley," Princess Sabrina cut in. "If the road is confusing and the path so easy to miss, it sounds like you will need him."

Finley sat back in the seat. "Then it's settled."

Demetra gaped at her sister in shock. As she climbed into the sleigh, she whispered, "I can't believe you took Finley's side."

"I'm not taking sides," Sabrina whispered back. "I just think two heads are better than one. And I don't want you to get lost, Demetra. Not when the guests are about to arrive for the Winterfest."

Demetra knew her sister was right. With a frustrated sigh, she picked up the reins and opened her mouth to give directions to the reindeer.

But Finley spoke first. "Rolf, let's take the back route along Glacier's Edge. It's much faster. Giddyup!"

As the reindeer clip-clopped across the frozen lake, Demetra turned and called to her sister, "See?"

Sabrina cupped her hands around her mouth and called, "Remember, work together!"

2

Trouble at Sparkle Mountain

When the princess and the fox reached
the foot of Sparkle Mountain, the cloud
had grown. It now covered the mountain
like a sickly green fog.

"Where is the path?" Demetra asked,
squinting through the mist.

Finley scampered forward onto Rolf's
back. "I'm not really sure," he called.

"Not sure!" Demetra huffed. "But you
said *you* were the only one who knew
how to find it!"

"I *would* know how to find it in good

weather," Finley shot back. "But right now, I can barely see my paw in front of my nose!"

"We had better go look for it," Demetra said, hopping out of the sleigh. Then she called to the reindeer, "Wait for us here, Rolf."

"As you wish, my lady," Rolf replied.

Demetra and Finley inched into the green mist. They hadn't gone more than ten feet when they froze. Someone was crying. Quite close by.

"I don't know what to do," a little voice moaned. "I'm such a coward."

"Someone's in trouble," Finley whispered.

The princess and the fox tiptoed

forward, following the sound. They climbed up a steep, snow-covered slope. Then they passed between two large boulders frosted over with pale green ice.

When Demetra and Finley found the owner of the voice, they nearly tripped over her. She was a tiny white bunny huddled in the middle of the path.

"Why, look, it's Alpenglow," Demetra cried.

The bunny looked up at the princess with frightened eyes. "I wanted to help but I couldn't," she whimpered.

"Help who?" the princess asked.

"Elsinor and the other Goblins," Alpenglow explained. "They're trapped inside Sparkle Mountain."

"What were they doing in there?" Finley asked.

"Mining for rock crystal," Alpenglow whimpered. "It was to be a surprise for you, Princess. In honor of Winterfest."

"Oh, dear," Demetra replied. "This is terrible. Can you tell us what happened?"

"I heard a loud crashing sound. Then the mountain started rumbling." Alpenglow sobbed, "I wanted to help the Goblins, but I was too frightened."

Demetra placed one hand on Alpenglow's head. The bunny was shaking so hard her teeth chattered. "There was nothing you could do," Demetra said gently. "Don't blame yourself."

"It sounds like they've had a cave-in," Finley whispered to Demetra.

The princess nodded. "Elsinor and his Goblins could be buried under the rocks."

"Use your Magic Mirror," Finley said, tugging on Demetra's arm.

"I planned on doing that," she replied.

Actually the news about the Goblins was so upsetting that Demetra had forgotten she was carrying the Magic Mirror.

"Look into it and see if the Goblins are hurt," the white fox urged.

"I will!"

Demetra didn't like it when Finley

barked orders at her. It made her flustered.

She fumbled for the Magic Mirror. It had been given to her by the great wizard Gallivant on the day she was crowned the Diamond Princess. The mirror gave Demetra the power to see people and things in other places.

Finley tugged on her sleeve again. "Remember, you can only use it three times in one day."

"I know that," Demetra snapped at Finley. He was starting to irritate her.

She took two steps away from him and raised the shimmering glass into the air. The diamonds on its handle sparkled in the mist.

*"Oh, Magic Mirror, so shiny bright,
Show me the Goblins. Are they all
right?"*

The silver mirror suddenly turned
into a reflecting pool. Demetra could see
Elsinor and two other lavender Goblins
huddled together on a large white
mound. Big rock crystals were scattered
around them.

"Can you see them?" Finley asked.

Demetra nodded. "They don't appear
to be hurt. But they look frightened."

"Where are they?" Finley asked.

"I'm not sure," Demetra said with a
frown. "They're surrounded by crystals."

"Can you see anything else?" Finley
asked.

Demetra looked back at the mirror, but the image had disappeared. "No."

"Well, what should we do?" Finley asked.

Demetra pursed her lips. "We have to go in," she said finally.

"But how do you plan to get inside?" Finley waved his paw in the mist. "We can't even see the mine entrance."

Alpenglow raised herself up on her hind legs and pointed. "It's right behind you."

"Oh!" Finley spun quickly, then backed away from the big wooden door.

"What's the matter?" Demetra asked.

Finley stared at the mine entrance. "Ever since I was a little kit, I was warned never to go into Sparkle

Mountain. Something awful hides inside there."

"Like what?" Demetra whispered.

Finley twisted his fluffy tail nervously in his paws. "I'm not sure. But I hear terrible things happen to you if you go inside."

Demetra was surprised. Finley, who was usually so cocky, actually sounded frightened.

"Elsinor and the Goblins weren't afraid to go inside the mountain," Demetra pointed out.

"And look what happened to them," Finley rasped.

Finley's words made little goosebumps creep up Demetra's arms.

"Listen, Finley," she said, taking a

deep breath. "If it scares you so much, I'll go into the mountain by myself. You can wait with Alpenglow and Rolf in the sleigh."

"I am *not* scared," Finley sputtered. He puffed up his chest, trying to act brave. "And I will *not* wait in the sleigh. I'm going with you. In fact," he added, marching into the mist, "I'll lead the way."

3

Hunting for Goblins

Two tunnels lay behind the wooden door. The one to the right was big and dark. The one to the left was much smaller but glistened with light.

"I think we should take the lighted tunnel," Demetra declared.

Finley shook his head firmly. "We have to be cautious, Princess. We don't know what's down there. We could get trapped. I say we take the big tunnel."

Demetra put her hands on her hips. "But the big tunnel is so dark. We don't know what's down there either."

The fox rapped on the rock with his paw. "Yes, but this rock is solid. It would never collapse."

The princess peeked inside the black tunnel and shivered. It was dark. Demetra wouldn't admit it to Finley, but she was afraid of the dark.

"The little tunnel is bright and shiny," she declared. "I like that one."

"Well, I don't," Finley said stubbornly.

Demetra glared at the fox. "Then I guess I'll just have to use the Magic Mirror. It'll tell us which one to choose."

Before Finley could protest, Demetra raised the sparkling mirror above her head and chanted:

"Magic Mirror, so shiny bright,
Where is Elsinor, in dark or light?"

Once again the mirror became a liquid pool. And once again, Demetra saw Elsinor and the Goblins seated on a large white mound, looking miserable.

"We need to take the little tunnel," Demetra announced. "It's obvious."

Finley peered over her shoulder. "But that's the same picture you saw before. You just wasted a turn with the mirror. Now you only have one left."

"It doesn't matter," she said, as the image faded from view. "That was Elsinor, and he was clearly in the light. So I'm taking the lighted tunnel."

With one last glance at the big tunnel, Finley said, "Because I am your advisor and protector, I must go with you."

"Suit yourself."

Demetra led the way into the little tunnel. It *was* lighted, but the farther they traveled into it, the narrower it got. Pretty soon the princess was crawling on her hands and knees.

"I feel it's my duty to point out that you picked the wrong tunnel," Finley declared from behind her.

Demetra knew the fox was right, but she hated to admit it. She crawled forward in silence and bumped her head on the ceiling.

"I'll bet that hurt," Finley said. "If

we'd taken my way, we'd still be walking and your head would be fine."

Demetra rubbed the top of her head and grumbled, "You don't know that. Your tunnel could have been just as narrow."

Now Demetra was really having to struggle to fit through the passage. Her shoulders scraped against the walls, and she hit her head several more times against the ceiling.

"Oh, no," she moaned, as she turned a corner and nearly bumped into a stone wall that blocked the tunnel. "This is the end."

"What did I tell you?" Finley sang out.

Demetra's head hurt from hitting the

rock, and she knew she'd picked the wrong tunnel. But she didn't need Finley to rub it in.

"Why does it make you happy that you're right and I'm wrong?" she hissed at Finley.

"Happy?" Finley repeated. "I'm not at all happy. I'm concerned."

"You call that concern?" Demetra replied. "You point out every mistake I make!"

The white fox seemed genuinely surprised. "But that's my job. I'm the palace advisor."

"An advisor gives advice," Demetra declared. "He doesn't criticize."

"But you won't take my advice," he

replied. "Especially about the Winterfest. All you do is argue with me."

Finley was right. During the planning for the Winterfest he'd tried to give suggestions, but she'd fought most of them. But then he'd called her a name.

"Why did you call me a pigheaded little princess?" Demetra asked.

There was a long silence. Finally Finley said, "Because you had just called me a snotty little furball, and my feelings were hurt."

Demetra winced. She forgot she *had* called him a snotty furball. And a few other names. Now she wished she hadn't.

The princess opened her mouth to apologize, but something stopped her. A low rumbling sound filled the air.

Rrrrr!

"Did you hear that?" Finley asked.

Demetra nodded.

Rrrrr!

"There it is again!" Finley whispered. "It sounds like snoring."

"Or growling," Demetra whispered back.

They both gulped. Hard.

"It's coming from behind that wall." Finley pointed at the rock in front of them. "I told you something awful was inside this mountain."

Demetra instantly started crawling backwards. "You know, Finley," she said, in a very shaky voice, "you were right.

We *should* have taken the big tunnel."

Finley didn't answer. He had already turned and was running full tilt for the mine entrance.

"Finley!" Demetra cried, standing up and running after him. "Where are you going?"

"Home!" Finley called over his shoulder. "I'm sorry, Princess, but I just can't stay here another minute."

At the entrance, Finley dove for the door.

But Demetra was too fast for him. She caught hold of his tail and cried, "You can't leave. We have to save Elsinor and the others."

Finley clung to the handle of the big

oak door with both paws. "Don't make me!"

"Finley, please!" Demetra tugged with all of her might. "I can't do it by myself."

"Why?"

Demetra looked at the pitch-black tunnel. "Because I'm afraid of the dark!"

This took Finley by surprise and he let go of the door. The two of them tumbled backwards into the blackness of the big rock tunnel.

The Long Dark Tunnel

"Yeow!" Demetra hit her head on the hard rock wall. For a second she saw stars. "That hurt!"

The big tunnel was pitch black and freezing cold. Demetra felt for the wall and pulled herself to her feet.

"Finley?" she called. "Are you all right?"

No answer.

"Finley!" She reached into the darkness in front of her. "Are you there?"

Still no answer.

The goose bumps returned. They crept up her arms and down the back of her neck.

"Finley?" she sang out in a quivery voice. "This isn't funny. You know I'm afraid of the dark. Now, please answer me."

She held her breath and listened. Nothing.

"Maybe Finley's hurt," she whispered, "and can't speak." She inched forward. "Don't worry, Finley. I'll find you."

The princess spread her arms out to the sides and waved them above her head. "This tunnel is enormous," she murmured. "Something very large could live in here."

The thought of something very large actually being in the tunnel with her made Demetra's heart thud faster.

"Of course," Demetra called in a high voice, "if something large *was* in here, it would let me know. Wouldn't it?"

She waited for an answer. But none came.

"Good." The princess heaved a sigh of relief. "For a moment there, I thought Finley's story about the scary thing inside the mountain might be true."

She chuckled to herself, turned, and froze.

Just ahead was a thin beam of light. It stretched from the ceiling to the tunnel floor.

"That must be some kind of window to outside," Demetra murmured.

But the light didn't just touch the floor. It went *through* it. If Demetra had been looking down, she would have noticed that.

Instead, her head was tilted upward as she stepped into the beam of light. "Sky!" she gasped. "That looks like—helllllllllp!"

Demetra tumbled through the large hole in the tunnel floor.

Glowing crystals sparkled all around the princess. They were as bright as stars on a clear night.

Demetra held her breath, waiting to crash into the hard rock.

But just as she was about to hit the ground, two large hands reached out for her.

They were bright purple and covered in tiny green spots.

5

The Crystal Cave

"Caught you!" a male voice croaked, as Demetra fell into his outstretched arms. "Princess, are you all right?"

The green mist was thicker than ever, and Demetra could hardly see.

"Elsinor?" she asked, leaning her face closer to her rescuer's. "Is that you?"

The Goblin leader had bright red eyes, two pointed lavender ears, and a bushy tuft of green hair that exploded out of the top of his head.

He smiled at her, revealing two large

fangs. "At your service, milady."

"Have you seen Finley?" Demetra asked, as Elsinor set her onto the soft white ground. "We were in a dark tunnel and I lost him."

"I'm here," Finley called, limping through the mist. "I fell through that, too. But I'm not sure where *here* is."

"I believe we're at the heart of Sparkle Mountain," a small, round Goblin named Crag replied. "We fell into this Crystal Cave this morning."

"How did it happen?" Demetra asked.

"We were mining for crystal in that big, dark tunnel," Elsinor explained, "when Tor broke a hole through the rock."

Tor nodded vigorously. "The floor

crumbled around our feet. I fell through the hole first. Then Crag, then Adit, and finally everyone followed me."

Elsinor stomped his foot on the soft white ground. "We landed on this strange hill."

"And we've been stuck here ever since," Crag finished.

"There must be some way to get out of here," Finley said, scanning the sparkling walls of the cave. "A door or a crack in the crystal."

Elsinor shook his head. "We've looked. The only way out is the way we came in." He pointed upward. "Through that hole."

Demetra looked up. She could see the

opening in the roof of the cave. Beyond that, at the end of a long narrow shaft, she could just glimpse a bit of blue.

"Is that the sky?" she asked.

"Yes," Adit replied. "That's an air shaft. We used it to send for help."

"You mean you made that green cloud?" Finley asked.

"With this." Elsinor showed them a small glass bottle of glowing green liquid.

"He mixed peridot ore with water to create a mist," Crag explained. "Then we fanned it through that hole."

"Your signal worked," the princess said. "We saw the green cloud and rushed to see what was the matter."

"But the fog was so thick, we could barely find the path up the mountain," Finley added.

Elsinor smiled sheepishly. "I wasn't sure how much ore to use." He coughed, and batted at the mist swirling around his face. "I'm afraid I overdid it."

Finley leaned forward and whispered, "I've always heard that something very large and very frightening lives inside this mountain."

"I've heard that story, too," Elsinor whispered back. "But I've never seen anything."

"I'm very glad to hear it," Finley said, putting one paw to his heart.

Suddenly the mound trembled.

"What's going on?" Demetra cried, her teeth clattering together. "It feels like an earthquake."

"Don't panic," Crag said, as he steadied the princess with one purple hand. "Sometimes the ground will shake for minutes at a time."

"And sometimes it makes a deep rumbling noise," Tor added. "Like snoring."

"Finley and I heard that sound before," Demetra said. "I wonder what it is."

The Diamond Princess bent down and touched the white grass at her feet. "You know, this doesn't feel like grass. It feels more like fur."

Finley patted the ground with his paws. "You're right."

The princess crawled away from the group, patting the fur as she went.

"Careful, Princess," Elsinor called through the mist. "You might slip off the hill and cut yourself on the crystal."

"I'll protect you," Finley said, hurrying to join the princess.

Demetra crawled up a furry hill and down a narrow slope. Suddenly her hand touched something cold and rubbery.

"Oh," she murmured, "this feels odd. Like a very large . . . nose."

Demetra stretched both hands over the edge of it and grasped something smooth and pointed. "And this feels like a very sharp . . . tooth."

"A hill doesn't have a nose or teeth," Finley murmured.

"Oh, Finley!" Demetra quickly backed up the slope. "This isn't a hill. It's a . . . It's a . . . "

Suddenly the white ground they were standing on rose into the air, lifting them almost to the ceiling.

"BEAR!"

6

It's a Bear!

"Who is it that wakes me from my slumber?" the Big Bear roared.

Demetra, Finley, and the Goblins clung to the beast's fur but didn't answer.

"Tell me who you are!" the Big Bear bellowed. "And be quick about it. I'm very tired and very hungry."

"Hungry?" Finley gasped. "Yikes!"

Elsinor spoke first. "I am Elsinor, leader of the Goblins."

The Big Bear threw back his head and howled, "Did Lord Bleak send you?"

"Lord Bleak?" Demetra repeated. "You know him?"

"Bleak rules this kingdom," the Big Bear replied.

"Oh, no," Demetra said. "Queen Jemma and King Regal rule the Jewel Kingdom now. They sent Bleak away. He's far across the Black Sea."

The Big Bear slowly turned his head so his big black eyes were level with Demetra. "Who are you?"

Demetra tilted her chin up, trying to look as royal as possible. "I am Princess Demetra, the Diamond Princess. My parents rule the Jewel Kingdom. And I rule the White Winterland."

The Big Bear's eyes narrowed. "I don't believe you."

"Just ask anybody," Finley called from behind the princess. "They'll tell you it's true."

"I see no one," the Big Bear snarled. "I speak to no one. I sleep here in this cave, a prisoner of Lord Bleak."

"Lord Bleak must have walled him in here years ago," Elsinor whispered to the princess.

"Poor fellow," the princess whispered back.

"I wouldn't feel sorry for him," Finley hissed. "He must have done something terrible to be taken prisoner."

"What are you whispering about?" the Big Bear demanded.

"N-n-nothing, Mr. Bear, sir," Finley stammered. "We were just saying how this is all an unfortunate accident. We didn't mean to fall into your cave. So if you would just help us get out of here, we promise never to return."

"No one leaves this cave alive!" The Big Bear roared so loudly his body shook.

"But why?" Demetra asked, losing her balance and falling to her knees.

"If I let one of you step foot outside this cave, you'll tell Lord Bleak I am free. And ready to fight him again."

"But there is no Lord Bleak!" Finley cried. "He's gone!"

"You're lying!" The Big Bear swiped at the white fox with a giant clawed foot. "I don't like liars."

Finley tried to duck but the blow knocked him off the bear's back. He lay on the crystal floor, pinned beneath the Big Bear's paw.

"The bear's got Finley!" Crag cried. "What should we do?"

"Whatever it is, we'd better be quick about it," Elsinor warned. "He's crushing Finley."

Demetra didn't even pause to think. She leaped off the Big Bear's back and landed with a loud *thump* on the cave floor.

"Release him!" she commanded. "I can prove that Lord Bleak no longer rules this land."

The Big Bear narrowed his eyes. "You can? How?"

"With my Magic Mirror." Demetra

pulled the mirror from inside her jacket.

"Careful, Princess," Finley choked from under the Big Bear's paw. "You've already used the mirror twice. This is your last time."

"I know that," Demetra whispered back.

The princess held the sparkling mirror in front of the Big Bear's nose. "Well?"

The bear stared at the mirror for a long time. "All right," he said finally. "Prove it."

"I will," Demetra said. "On one condition."

The bear squinted one eye closed. "What?"

"That you let us go."

The Big Bear considered this for a moment. "I'll let this fox and those Goblins go," he replied. "But you, Princess, must stay."

Princess Demetra looked quickly at Finley, who was gasping for air under the bear's paw.

If she agreed, she might never see her friends and family again. But if she didn't, the bear would destroy Finley.

"All right," Demetra said with a gulp. "I'll stay."

7

The Magic Mirror

The Big Bear lifted Elsinor and the Goblins through the hole in the cave ceiling. Then he turned to Finley.

"You're next," the Big Bear growled, reaching for the small white fox.

But Finley shook his head.

"If Princess Demetra stays, then I stay," he said boldly.

"Finley," Demetra hissed between clenched teeth. "This is no time to be stubborn. Leave this cave and run for help."

"Elsinor can do that," Finley whispered back. "My place is with you, my friend. Whatever happens to you happens to me."

Demetra's eyes filled with tears. "Oh, Finley, that's really very sweet."

Finley shrugged. "It's the least I can do for calling you a pigheaded princess."

"But I *was* pigheaded," Demetra confessed. "And bossy."

Finley twisted his fluffy white tail in his paws. "Well . . . maybe just a little."

"Ahem!" The Big Bear cleared his throat. "Aren't you two forgetting something?"

"Sorry?" Demetra blinked her large blue eyes.

"The Magic Mirror," the Big Bear growled impatiently. "You were going to show me Lord Bleak."

"No," the princess corrected. "I was going to show you my parents, King Regal and Queen Jemma. They're the rulers of the Jewel Kingdom."

The Bear slammed one huge paw onto the ground, spraying bits of broken crystal everywhere. "I want to see Lord Bleak!"

Demetra had never seen Lord Bleak, but she had heard that he was awful to look at. He once had been handsome, but the evil inside him twisted his features into an ugly mask.

"I don't know if I can stand to look at

him," she replied in a tiny voice. "Maybe *you* should use the mirror."

She offered the glittering mirror to the Big Bear.

He reached for it, then quickly withdrew his paw. "What is this?" he snarled, "some kind of trick? I'm not touching that mirror."

"You can touch it," Demetra assured the Big Bear. "It won't hurt you."

To prove it, Finley reached for the shimmering glass. "See? It's easy." He raised the mirror in the air and explained, "You simply say, *Magic Mirror so shiny bright*, then wish for something you'd like to see."

"That's right," Demetra nodded.

With the mirror still in the air, Finley said, "I'll tell you what I'd like to see. I'd like to see the Winterfest Parade. With all of our friends from the White Winterland. If I could just have one last glimpse of them, I'd be happy."

Suddenly the diamonds on the handle began to sparkle. And the mirrored glass turned into a silver reflecting pool.

"Finley!" Demetra gasped. "What have you done? That was the third wish. There are no more."

Finley slowly turned to face the Big Bear. He held out the Magic Mirror and murmured, "Oops!"

8

Join the Parade!

The Big Bear was about to smash the Magic Mirror against a rock when something he saw stopped him.

"That looks like my old friend, Charger," he murmured. "But that's not possible."

Princess Demetra peered over his paw at the image in the mirror. A white winged horse was leading a parade of people carrying torches and silver banners.

"That *is* Charger," Demetra cried.

"He's leading the Winterfest Parade. Oh, look!" she gasped, pointing to the three princesses behind the winged horse. "Those are my sisters Roxanne, Emily, and Sabrina."

The Big Bear turned to her in amazement. "Charger is my oldest and dearest friend. Together we tried to stop Lord Bleak. But we couldn't do it." The Big Bear looked back at the image. "We were separated when Bleak took us prisoner. I thought Charger was dead."

"Charger escaped," Finley explained. "He fought twenty of Bleak's terrible Darklings to do it." The fox pointed at the horse in the mirror. "You can see his battle scars there, across his chest."

"So what you say is true," the Big Bear gasped. "Lord Bleak is banished."

Demetra nodded vigorously. "He's far across the Black Sea."

"And the evil Darklings?"

"They were packed off with him," Finley added. "Now everyone in our kingdom is free and happy."

"Then I can come out," the Big Bear said softly.

"And see your friends," Demetra added. "You're free now."

Two huge teardrops formed in the Big Bear's eyes. Finley and Demetra managed to leap out of the way as the tears dripped off the tip of his nose and splashed onto the cave floor.

"Oh, dear," Demetra exclaimed. "I hope those aren't tears of sadness."

"Oh, no," the Big Bear said, shaking his head. "They are tears of joy. How I've dreamed of this day! But I never thought it would happen."

Finley, who was busy watching the action in the mirror, suddenly said, "I thought the parade was supposed to circle the lake and return to the castle."

"It is," Demetra replied.

"Well, they've left the lake," Finley observed. "And now they're marching up here. Toward Sparkle Mountain."

"Look at their faces," Demetra said. "They don't look happy. They look worried."

"Look at Charger," the Big Bear added. "He's no longer marching, he's flying. And one of those purple Goblins is on his back."

"They're coming to rescue us!" Demetra cried. She looked at Finley and whispered, "We made a promise to stay here with the Big Bear. We've got to stop them."

"Why stop them?" the Big Bear declared, rearing up on his hind legs. With his huge paw he punched a bigger hole in the cave's roof. "Let's join them."

"You mean we are free to go?" Finley asked.

The Big Bear chuckled, "Of course. We're all free!"

Then he reached behind a crystal boulder and pulled out a big red collar. It was studded with sparkling diamonds.

"Help me put this on, will you?" he asked, dropping it in front of Demetra. "I want to look my best when I greet Charger."

Demetra read the name on the collar. "Bernard. Is that your name?"

"Why, yes it is," the Big Bear replied, with a bow of his head. "Bernard Bear. And I am very pleased to make your acquaintance, Princess Demetra. And yours, too, Mr. Finley."

While Bernard Bear told his tale of being imprisoned in the Crystal Cave and sleeping for years, Finley and

Demetra worked to make him look presentable.

They buckled the collar around his neck. Then Demetra untangled the knots in his fur. And Finley smoothed the hair around his face.

When they'd finished, Demetra clapped her hands together. "Oh, Bernard, you look magnificent!"

"Why, thank you, my lady." Bernard replied. "Now if you two will climb onto my back, we'll join the parade."

"Will we have to go back through that dark tunnel?" Demetra asked.

Bernard nodded his huge head. "It's the only way out."

Demetra gulped.

"Don't worry, Princess," Finley whispered. "I'll hold your hand."

Demetra smiled at the fox and murmured, "Thanks, friend."

Minutes later, Bernard Bear appeared at the mine entrance. Princess Demetra and Finley were waving merrily from his back.

The cheer that rose up from the waiting crowd was deafening.

A shrill whinny split the air as Charger recognized his old friend and flew to meet Bernard.

Once Demetra and Finley were safely on the ground, Princess Sabrina rushed forward. She was followed by Emily and Roxanne.

"Are you all right?" Sabrina cried breathlessly.

"We were so worried," Emily said, hugging Demetra.

"When Elsinor told us that a giant bear was holding you prisoner," Roxanne cut in, "we came as fast as we could."

"We were afraid the bear might have eaten you," Sabrina said with a frown.

"Oh, no," Demetra chuckled. "He would'nt do that. He doesn't like meat."

"Bernard told us he only eats fruits and nuts," Finley added. "And I must say I was very glad to hear that."

Sabrina looked from Demetra to Finley. And back again. Finally she asked, "You and Finley? Are you . . . ?"

"Are we what, Sabrina?" Demetra asked with a twinkle in her eye.

"Are you still . . . you know," Sabrina shrugged with frustration. "Fighting?"

Demetra and Finley looked at each other and started giggling.

"I believe I can answer your question," Finley said, taking Demetra by the hand. "Though the Diamond Princess can sometimes be a little pigheaded—"

"And though Finley has occasionally behaved like a snotty little furball," Demetra added. "We are now—"

"And will always be," Finley cut in.

They smiled at each other and declared, "Ever the best of friends!"

About the Authors

JAHNNA N. MALCOLM stands for Jahnna "and" Malcolm. Jahnna Beecham and Malcolm Hillgartner are married and write together. They have written over a hundred books for kids. Jahnna N. Malcolm have written about ballerinas, horses, ghosts, singing cowgirls, and green slime.

Before Jahnna and Malcolm wrote books, they were actors. They met on the stage where Malcolm was playing a prince. And they were married on the stage where Jahnna was playing a princess.

Now they have their own prince and princess: Dash and Skye. They all live in Oregon with their beautiful black dog, Glory, and their goofy hound, Huckleberry.

Visit www.jewelkingdom.com to learn more about Jahnna N. Malcolm and see pictures of the award-winning movie, *The Ruby Princess Runs Away.*